THE
PERSAIN
LOVER
By Natalie Patrón

TABLE OF CONTENTS

CHAPTER

CHAPTER I

Since 1979

In Tehran, Iran, an artist discovers a painting of the late Farah Pahlavi. He takes it home where he begins to distort the entire image. The beautiful, royal setting, the impeccable diamonds, even the color of her dark brown eyes he takes the liberty of covering in black while covering the rest of the canvas in blood red. Farah was the wife of the late Shah Mohammad Reza Pahlavi, the last Shah of Iran. The new, altered black and red interpretation of Farah offers the appearance of a symbol of a dark underground movement. It is so striking, in fact, copies of it wound up in many homes and public buildings.

Kohinoor, a petite, young, Iranian woman is shopping at The Grand Bazaar in the twelfth district of Tehran. She comes across a copy of the altered image of Farah and believes it would make a stunning addition to her Iranian lover's newly decorated home in The United States. She carefully wraps the bulky item and ships it around the world. The gift is received with great enthusiasm and her lover hangs the controversial print just above his fireplace.

In 2010 the U.S. Census tabulated a report of over a quarter of a million Iranians living in the United States. This calculation, however, only includes those who made a consorted effort to complete the documents. It is believed this number is under-representative of reality because "it does not include a total count of the number of individuals of Iranian ancestry in America."[1] Ninety percent of Iranians are devoted to Shi'i Islam; imagine the number of out of the quarter million that are Islam Extremists in the United States.

The entire culture is vastly different than the American one, from action to reaction. An article in the L.A. Times mentioned Robyn Wright's suggestion to Washington policy makers when approaching Iran. "Keep calm, do not react hastily above all do not reach for the gun."[2] Wright explains that "the U.S. is generally disliked because as a big power is assertive and intrusive and because its way of life is seductive and destructive of traditional culture and values."

Iranian President Hassan Rouhani stated "Many areas exist wherein these areas, it is possible many common interests exist."[3] An overlooked, double edged statement that seems to imply that residing in densely Persian populated communities within, America are sinister undertones. In addition, in 2014, Rouhani addressed the UN Assembly at which time he stated, "Certain Agencies have placed blades in the hands of mad men who now spare no one." He follows with, "Terrorism has become globalized."

With the overthrow of Mohammad Reza Shah Pahlavi in 1979, relations between the U.S. and Iran have become strained. Forget what you have heard on recent matters if you have not considered their history. If you have concerns that violence will break out between the two nations soon, you haven't been paying attention. According to the New York Post, war has already been waged against Americans and it goes back to the induction of the Republic of Islam.

---

[1] *iranianscount.org*

[2] *"Sacred Rage: The Wrath of Islam" by Robyn Wright*

[3] *Interview with 60 Minutes; September 2015*

From inception, Iran's new government underwent an overhaul taking with it:

52 Americans in the 1979 Tehran Hostage Crisis
17 Americans killed in the 1983 bombing of the U.S. Embassy in Beirut
241 Marines killed by the bombing of the Beirut Marine Barracks
5 Americans killed in the bombing of the Kuwait Embassy
The murder of CIA Station Chief, William F Buckley
2 Americans killed in terror attacks on Kuwaiti Airlines Flight 221
19 Serviceman killed in the 1996 Khobar Travers attack
American Lieutenant Colonel Leon James killed in Bagdad by an EID

Rouhani's U.N. speech is shouting it from the mountain top but it is becoming lost in translation. He eludes a deep, dark, devious devotion. "Extremists of the world have united and the call has gone out."

Stella Pilot believes she has decoded the mysteries behind Rouhani's disturbing speech. Her experience would imply that crimes are being silently executed in the name of Allah. These are not battlefield crimes, these are crimes against humanity. Human rights are being violated in our country. Our way of life is being used against us in a war waged on a government that we, as American citizens, don't even trust. These crimes are so well calculated that they sometimes take months to discover.

American women are being used as sheep, quite literally, and the words of warning for this are all provided in double-speak. Officials have us believing they are talking about one thing when in reality the advisory refers to something quite different. When dealing with these types of mental gymnastics, it becomes difficult to distinguish between the language of the criminal and the language of the sincere.

Pay attention to Stella's story of a specialized type of guerrilla warfare she trusts is taking place in our privileged neighborhoods. Her allegations make their way to a nationally recognized, federally funded, globally televised microphone. This operation does not require Uranium; it does not require explosives of any sort. No military is called upon and no money is exchanged. No oil is at risk and no economy is in jeopardy. No lives will be saved and no one will perish. There are victims, however and their lives will be changed forever in a way that contradicts the American culture. The wrath of three generations of angry Islam Extremists has been spoken of for decades. Stella considers the anticipation to be false; they are here, it is happening, now. Heed the words of The Ayatollah Mouhammed Rouhani: "Certain Agencies have placed razors in the hands of madmen who now spare no one."

CHAPTER II

An American Struggle

Falling to her knees as they said their goodbyes, Stella Pilot hung up the phone, stuffed back her tears and instead let out an incredible holler. It carried the sounds of frustration, anger and despair all of which she was feeling but her lunch break was over and she had to return to work. She instantly felt such distain for social media and the Internet. If she hadn't been dabbling on it during her lunch hour, maybe, just maybe, the door with Adam behind it wouldn't have slammed in her face today.

Adam was the very definition of Stella's rebound. She had divorced after a ten year marriage and purchased from Adam what she referred to as "her getaway car." Stella was a young, American beauty. She had a medium build and donned long, soft, golden blonde colored hair with intensively beautiful blue eyes that matched her angelic smile. Her skin was smooth and fair which was a stark contrast to her naturally thick, dark eyebrows. Stella's German heritage was exhibited in her overall stature; complete with a seemingly enhanced breast size that beautifully complimented her actually, but naturally, enhanced backside. Stella had lived in Santa Monica, California for the last thirteen years. She and her ex-husband had moved there to follow his career in engineering. The relocation turned out to benefit them both once Stella landed her position as the Marketing Manager at Coding Leaders, Inc.

Stella's courtship with the man she married had been motivated by sex; they both carried an insatiable appetite for it and she would have to leave him before she realized how he eventually used it as a weapon against her. While dating, their relationship was accompanied with many outlining red flags she treated as badges of honor rather than serious warnings about the future of their relationship. This is a mistake often made by lonely and broken girls who know in their hearts that things are not right.

Unfortunately, they have been taught that the ability to tolerate such injustices in the name of love is the strength it takes to overcome a challenge that would threaten something as serious as marriage. Stella was the poster child for these broken girls and it would turn out that no one in her life would point her in a different direction. In fact, everything in her life encouraged her directly into the dangers of a marriage that would slowly but certainly strangle the growth, creativity, joy, and even decision making out of her.

One day, Stella simply woke up and left him.

Adam was a car dealer in Santa Monica and had immediately caught Stella's eye at the same time she was leaving her ex-husband. Her pursuit of him was extensive. She spent months sending short, suggestive emails with her car payments in hopes of landing a date with him, and once it happened her heart took flight. She remembers how she could hardly contain her emotions when she heard from him. He seemed to be intrigued by her reservation in public and conflicting liberation in the bedroom. Adam was careful to cultivate their liaison to benefit his libido but kept her at arm's length when she tried to get close. He was so skilled at sales that he could convince her they were headed in the same direction just long enough to get her in bed one more time. This is what she allowed herself to believe was love.

Though their affair lasted only a few months, it would be a year and a half before Stella would be able to refrain from crying over him on a daily basis. A year went by and all of her vacation and sick time, available through work, were squandered away on tear filled marathons that littered her room with a collection of used tissues. With a new year come and gone, she faced, again, running dangerously slim on available time off from work for the same reason.

Stella, however, fell into such agony that she called in sick from work, once again, for three days in a row. This would end the work week and she would have the weekend as well to recover from her misery. That Friday, she was relieved that she remembered to call her office and let them know she had been summoned for jury duty the following Monday and would not, after all, be back in the office that day. The phone call made her nervous considering it had been made on the tail end of her hiatus.

Stella was indeed chosen to sit as a juror on a trial and it would be one that she would forever remember. She believed the defendant was innocent although he was accompanied by a lawyer who provided him with far less than a substantial defense. Stella took detailed notes and knew that the police were enhancing the truth to fit their case. In the juror's lounge, she was sure that it would be an easy decision. It turned out, however, Stella stood alone. The remainder of the jury had not kept the same notes that concluded the prosecution's inconsistencies. She was stubborn and clever and took her time – and theirs – planting several seeds of doubt and in time brought the whole jury around. They found the man innocent and Stella would forever feel that she saved him from a bully in a uniform.

That same night, Stella came down with a stomach virus and a fever that kept her awake. It landed her such frequent trips to the bathroom that eventually she set up camp on the cold, tiled floor. When the sun started peeking through the window, Stella could barely see from behind the blinding headache she had developed. She scooped herself off the floor and stumbled to the bedroom to find her phone. She placed another call, filled with apologies, but that she just simply couldn't make it into work that day. The call wasn't received well though she didn't have a minute to think about it once she became woozy from the pumping adrenaline in her veins.

The next day, Stella's health had improved dramatically. She returned to the office only to find the atmosphere had been replaced. No one would speak, smile or even look at her. It was as if she were the walking dead. Around the lunch hour, she took a phone call from her landlord saying there was a fire in the building and asked if she could come home. She grabbed her things and cited that she was taking her lunch break and drove home as fast as she could. Since no one had been speaking to her that day, she didn't stick around for any sort of response or reaction to her announcement.

By the time she arrived, the fire had been doused. The landlord was in the parking lot explaining to a group of tenants the cause of the fire and the details of the dramatic event. Stella didn't stop to join them and instead walked straight into the smoldering building to perceive the damage endured on her small, 600 square foot space. Everything large had pretty much been devoured by either fire or smoke. Her front hallway closet had been spared and thankfully the contents of it included family photos, her birth certificate and a collection of books; the rest was replaceable. With haste, she put together a few items of clothing that escaped irrevocable damage before any authorities came in to tell her to leave and she returned to work as quickly as she had left.

As she made her way to her desk, her supervisor asked Stella to join her in the Vice President's office. Once, inside, she already knew what was in front of her. The presentation was swift and mind numbing as her authorities at Coding Leaders, Inc. expressed that her relationship with her job had been terminated. They backed up their decision with examples of her recent stretch of absences which had unfortunately coincided with an important client event. The room was silent for some time but Stella was fighting off an agonizing ring in her ears. She wondered if they cared to know about the fire that had just consumed her home. The blaze's ashes were still smoking as she sat in the square, glass fish bowl office. As the ring faded, she looked the Vice President squarely in the eye and said, "Thank you for the opportunity." And that is how Stella, in the blink of an eye, became homeless and unemployed.

That evening, once she had gathered everything she could salvage from her charred apartment, she checked into a hotel just down the street. As she rummaged through what her life possessions now amounted to, she began to experience the familiar ringing in her ears that had plagued her during the execution at her now previous job. Stella could not understand at the moment why so much destruction had bestowed her and all at once. She took advantage of the silent space to sob at an accelerated volume.

The loss of important bedrock pillars such as a house or an income, for a properly conditioned American mind, produces such trauma that almost guarantees the personality of someone who suffers such a loss, will forever be altered. Studies show that the removal of just one of these pillars in a person's life is enough to induce a mental breakdown. To experience two of these foundational dislocations simultaneously, had definite potential for the onset of mental destruction.

To someone like Stella, who had become familiar with the world crumbling around her at a very early age, it was another ride in the eye of the storm. Experience and repetition of a world flipping upside down provided her with the ability to become astutely calm when such situations arose. At times, others marveled at her steady and stable demeanor in the face of incredibly challenging conditions. She noticed as she aged that these storms had become larger and larger. Stella knew she was capable of taking this kind of "hit" too. She was so well acquainted with chaos that the worse it became, the greater her ability to remain calm grew.

Without the assistance of an income, Stella had to act quickly. She wasn't going to be able to remain in a hotel very long but her new unemployment would make it impossible to rent another apartment. Stella's close friend, whom she had known since college, graciously offered her spare bedroom to stay in while she found a job and got back on her feet.

"It will be just like the old days." Her friend encouraged.

The two lived down the hall from each other in the same apartment building in the small town they went to school. They would often walk in and out of each other's house freely and Stella thought this would be a soft landing spot for her newfound challenge.

Hours were spent scouring jobs and filling out applications. She would obtain HR names and numbers, call them to introduce herself ask for her own interviews and her tenacity landed her several of them. For as proficient as she was at the process of finding a job, there had been a shift in her that was apparent during each of these interviews that was holding her back from landing any of them. For her, it was clear as day but society was providing a struggle that would keep her from her true calling. The employers could feel the insincerity of her desire and she would not receive an offer.

Finally, she decided she was not using her time wisely. She was not landing jobs because that wasn't the life she was hoping for. She wanted to live the American Dream, achieve financial freedom and not work for wages. This would mean taking control of her life in a whole new way. Without her ex-husband as an excuse for delaying this process any longer, she began to make lists of things to do on a daily basis.

The lists were overwhelming at first but once she learned to break them down, she quickly had a firm grasp on time management. With her new monthly struggle to pay any sort of rent, she felt she was failing constantly. This burden swelled when her friends informed her that they unfortunately needed the room back. Her friend's dad would be having surgery and they would have him there for his recovery. The temporary solution that had been provided had expired and she was right back where she started two months prior.

Fortunately, Stella was able to find an apartment to sublet for a few months and this would buy her a little more time but would dwindle away her savings. This was alright with her, for she felt grateful to have a roof over her head. In an attempt to take control of her time, Stella began brainstorming a new business idea. There was money out there to be made and she wanted to find out how others were doing it.

With her new apartment, the burden of income became dire but this was quickly solved when the friend whom she had been staying with informed her of a contract position she had landed for catering at a country club. She offered Stella a partnership in the contract and suddenly Stella had recovered from life having kicked the ever loving daylights out of her. This would also put Stella's new business idea on hold.

The partnership came with early mornings and late nights but this didn't bother either one of them because they were so happy to have become their own bosses. The contract at the kitchen ran into the holiday season and the instant success of the position consumed them both. Their clients included a weekday lunch for country club patrons and they also ran the catering services for the kitchen which were available when the club rented out banquet rooms. This made for such extensive and exhaustive hours. They were working close to 18 hour days taking active charge of the entire process from preparation to cleanup. Even the planning, shopping and budget were included in their daily tasks.

Though the financial benefits were making the demands seem easier to maintain, there was always some sort of drama happening at the club. Often, Stella and her friend in the kitchen, who truly just wanted to make everyone happy by making good food, found themselves under fire for not spending more time at the country club during their off hours to socialize. Too much of this ambushing became tiresome to Stella who had come to a point in her life where she felt she didn't have to tolerate it. After the holidays, she voluntarily cut her hours and freed up some creative time for planning the business she was dreaming about before the contract with the country club came along. Research indicated that she could finance, with her tax refund, a license to run a food cart.

She poured herself into the design and foundation. It was an exciting experience for her to channel her talents into a project that was so personal. Her business cards, logo, slogan and website encompassed all of her spare time. She had developed a hot dog cart and called it "Captain's Crowd Pleasers." She bought a used cart off of the Internet and designed the unit on her own. The entire theme was nautical and she had even ordered a Sea Captain's uniform to wear as she sold her gourmet hot dogs. All she needed were a few minor changes to the website, a contracted location and then she would be ready to open for business.

CHAPTER III

Hollandaise

Two years ago, Stella's friend had told her about a swinger's club that she had been to with her husband and was almost certain Stella would enjoy. The delay in this was her aversion to going places alone but the admission to The Ruby Rabbit was so expensive for couples that Stella's friends always made excuses not to go with her. It was truly a sophisticated clientele and her friend thought she would fit right in. The original suggestion was made when Stella first began to complain of her agony without the constant sex that her marriage had provided. The divorce had been final for over two years now and the drought stirred up the courage to give the club a try. Some have even said that she took to it like a fish to water.

The extraordinary newfound income afforded her the opportunity to frequent the adult club where she grew to know certain couples as her friends. The exhausting weeks and lack of time on the weekends while she satisfied her new addiction infused Stella's ego rather than wear her down. She rode the high of the attention she received at The Ruby Rabbit all week long while she worked. Though her body was exhausted, her mind relived fantasy after fantasy and provided an energy that appeared supernatural.

She, quickly, fell prey to an older man who cried wolf about a broken heart. He told her that he had recently been dumped by a girl who was even younger than Stella's tender age of 33. The two became engaged in conversation. His name was Ron and he disclosed his age of 55 as they courted one another. This shocked her and she was deceived by having assumed a man his age just might be interested in more than a one night stand. This would quickly turn out to be a mistake in assumption that may have avoided some later frustration.

They moved to the basement and closed behind them a curtain to create a private room. The Ruby Rabbit had a myriad of beds and couches and cushions for people to retreat to when the time was right. The rooms in the basement were dark and empty with the exception of a mirror and a bed whose sheets were changed each time people left the space. Regardless of any future relationship, the two currently held in common their reason for being there. Slowly and seriously, he undressed them both while he maintained eye contact and provided gratuitous kisses.

Aware of his age, Stella paid close attention to his taste in love making. He proved to be quite old fashioned as he removed her clothes piece by piece. He revealed his Hispanic stature which was covered in dark and grey hairs. His chest was larger than average with toned muscle obviously built inside a gym and he smelled of leather and peppermint. Ron's erection was much bigger than her racial generalization had anticipated and she grabbed it with both hands and began to make love to his member with her mouth. He enjoyed this, letting out an uncontrollable gasp and grabbing the back of her head violently to make her stop almost immediately. He told her she was quite intense and that it was almost too much for him to handle. He paused a few moments before he had her lie down on the bed while he buried his face in her pussy to arouse her and distract himself.

After some time, Ron climbed on top of Stella and inserted his still hard cock. He was quiet with predictable enthusiasm and he moved with a pace that matched his age. Stella sensed that Ron's experiences were probably from a different generation and that if she were going to arrive at any sort of satisfaction from it, she would have to take charge. She asked Ron if she could have a turn on top. Once she climaxed, she dismounted him and posed on her knees as she motioned for him to kneel behind her. Stella's experience granted her knowledge of the pleasure that Ron's size alone would bring in this position.

He asked her a dozen times if she had climaxed which had always been a very disturbing question, drenched in selfishness, that made her annoyed and as a result provoked her to ignore him. Ron persisted until Stella couldn't stand the inquisition anymore and delivered to him the confirmation he was demanding; although, she knew this meant the end of the ride. As predicted, Ron heard her say yes and dug in his heels as he ramped up for his own finale. He resituated his knees behind her, grabbed both of her shoulders and thrust his hips as hard and as fast as he was able in the race to his finish. Stella still giggles about how he muttered the words, "Yep, it's comin' up" as the announcement of his climactic arrival.

Within minutes of their encounter, Ron asked her if she felt any connection to him or did she want to leave things as a one night stand. Although she did not feel any connection to him, she thought it would be interesting to see if this older gentleman could possibly be serious. He immediately asked her for a date. They went out only a few times before she caught on without reasonable doubt that he, in fact, was nothing more than an old man with a really good game. She swiftly and violently threw a fit when breaking up with Ron but immediately and all at once decided not to care. Rather, she began to realize that she was actually grateful for her short time with him. He did her a true favor by detaching the hook that Adam had held on her since his departure.

After the disappointment over "Ron-gate," Stella decided to reclaim the path she was previously on. She wasn't going to allow a possible encounter with him keep her from the adventure she was seeking. Her life, however, wasn't letting up. She still worked quite hard and in turn played even harder. Precious hours that she wasn't working she spent taking care of the home she felt she might lose at any minute. Laundry and dishes and tidiness altogether was not her strong suit.

One day, while at the grocery store - and not looking particularly well put together either - she found herself stuck behind an old woman who was having a hard time getting out of the way. Stella patiently waited and without concern for she had already become distracted by a man walking into the store. She scanned the individual and her eyes locked on this man with whom she was most impressed. He had sun-kissed brown skin, dark, mysterious eyes and he was wearing a baseball cap. His smile, as he spoke a foreign language on his phone, lit up the entire room around him. As he walked closer, her eyes did not leave him.

He seized up the situation about the traffic jam the elderly woman was causing and when his eyes met Stella's, he smiled in delight to find that she was not throwing a fit nor were her feathers even ruffled. Soon the elderly woman was able to steer her heavy cart in the right direction clearing a path. He moved past Stella and as he hung up his phone, he reached out and grabbed her arm and said, "So patient." His comment confirmed that she had been likewise noticed by him which excited Stella in a truly genuine way. She started to wish she had put herself together better before coming to the store that day.

As they scoured the aisles they seemed to meet over and over again. He taunted,

"It's the patient girl."

Each time they passed each other. She seized him up with an unabashed rubberneck pointed in his direction and smiled at him with a desire she believed he would never know about. The two of them could tell they equally enjoyed the flirting being exchanged and this fueled both of their confidence. Sometime later, she found him hunting for a packet of Hollandaise mix. Stella remembered looking for this item once too.

"You'll have to go to the other location on Main St. for that, they don't carry it here."

She offered without considering her imposition. The gorgeous man she had been flirting with looked at her directly, smiled grandly, thanked her and then continued shopping. A few minutes later, he approached her with his bags in hand. He said he had been on his way out of the store when he decided he must get to know the girl with such patience. He said,

"I would like to have your number."

Stella blushed at the idea of this man's apparent, genuine offer to get to know her even though she wasn't looking or feeling particularly well put together.

"Oh! You're shy?!" He exclaimed.

"No, you just made me blush."

"So…Can I have your number?"

"Yes, you can have my number. What is your name?" She asked.

"Raj." He replied.

"Raj?" She repeated.

"Yes, R-A-J."

It surprised her how similar his name was to Ron's.

"And what is your name?" He asked while extending his hand.

"Stella." She replied taking his hand gently.

"What is your nationality, Raj?" Stella asked, she was dying to know where his exotic accent originated.

"I am Persian, I'm from Iran." Raj answered and kissed her hand as he prepared to leave.

"Nice to meet you, Stella, I look forward to seeing you." He said with impeccable manners.

"Nice to meet you too." She answered, handed him her number and went home feeling youthful and hopeful that perhaps she had met a person willing to know Stella for who she really was.

Later that day, Raj sent a text message that read,

"Hey Stella, it was a pleasure to meet you, loved your smile and I'm glad we connected. Have a wonderful rest of the day and I'll catch you later   Raj…"

It made her glad to know this stranger took pride in his formal language over text messaging. It had always felt like an immature irritant that most people took part in a broken, digital language.

"Where RU going 2nite?" Drove her mad.

She responded soon after,

"Hi Raj, the pleasure was mine. I look forward to

22

hearing from you soon. Enjoy your weekend! ~Stella"

The hope of a man who was genuine was Stella's only driving force to follow through on a date with Raj. After all, it seemed so silly. How old could he be, she wondered? It didn't seem like his age was much different than that of 55 year old Ron, whom she had been recently duped by and who also coincidentally carried many features similar to this new man. They were both of darker complexion, both with shorter statures, receding hair lines and both with refreshingly terrific hygiene. But how would she get past their names, Ron and Raj? It made her want to look around for a hidden camera. Because they were so similar, should she discriminate against Raj for it? Or does she not force Raj to pay for Ron's indiscretions?

Society would indicate that she give Raj the benefit of the doubt. Psychologist all over the world would insist that to reject Raj due to a bad experience with Ron would be "misdirecting her emotions." To the contrary, Stella's instincts were barking at her and she wondered if the similarities of the two weren't a God given gift to steer her clear from familiar heartache. The internal conflict became a true struggle. Stella wasn't one to shy away from new experiences but this billboard sized sign from the universe wasn't allowing her to get past her disappointment in Ron. It created an instant suspicion in her about Raj that wasn't fair nor was it justified. This battle inside her would allow her to determine in advance that the upcoming date with Raj would be just that. There would be no future encounters after that. She decided that no matter what happened, they would simply have dinner and part ways.

With all this on her mind, it didn't bother her in the least that they struggled to connect and schedule this date. He made a few attempts to call and her return calls weren't reaching him either. Finally, their text messages met and they were able to work out getting together the following Saturday for dinner. Once or twice he tried moving the date to Friday but her work schedule at the country club would consume all her energy by Friday night. Beginning Thursday morning, they would have to cater both breakfast and lunch as well as serve regular individual lunch orders. The same schedule faced them

Friday. There would be no way she could enjoy herself on a Friday night.

Determined, he crafted a linguistic dream. His translation was a bit off but she had been able to tell by his dreamy accent that English was not his first language. At first, he tried simply asking but when she refused he made a valiant second attempt to meet on Friday. He attached a picture of a cherry blossom and wrote:

"Happy Friday! I am lobbying to have you join me for dinner and amazing fun tonight. I appreciate that it might be tough tonight but I am hoping you would give it a hard try. Wow factor awaits you."

And he stamped the message with an analog emoticon; colon, hyphen and closing parenthesis. She loved the chase he was initiating and basked in the attention but felt she had so many options beyond a man who might very well be as old as her father and made no concessions for him. Before the actual date, they texted a few more times, each testing the other's wit and sense of humor. The two were an extraordinary match. He incited the pretentious language with colorful zingers and she would craft elaborate responses to essentially egg him on. She felt quite domineering by Saturday night and was convinced that it was a shame he was so clever and fun since they would only be spending this one evening together.

Stella wanted to get serious about men and thought this man would make a good test run on how to say "no." She wasn't sure she would get to practice because he was probably too old fashioned for the type of date she was used to anyway. They had, after all, met in a grocery store and not a swinger's club. She didn't foresee this man making any sort of inappropriate advance on her. There would be no need for her to be delivered from the temptation of a man's intoxicating elixir. It would be an easy going evening for her.

She responded to what would be his last attempt to reschedule:

"I can see you are quite skilled at persuasion, however, I possess great powers of resistance and so shall defeat your exotic magnetism."

Raj conceded and bid her praises for her creative composition of speech; he would wait until Saturday.

CHAPTER IV

I Give You the Moon!

Saturday morning arrived and Stella was only slightly concerned that she was still spotting from her period. If her date with Raj went well, this could prove to be quite an inconvenience. She shook her head at herself, what was she worried about? She had already decided this would be an intellectual encounter not a physical one. She giggled a little to think she should be starting this habit on her first date of the New Year. Would she be able to see new results in her life by changing this one poor, habit?

It was quite a snowstorm outside that day and as the evening rolled in, Stella sent Raj a text and asked if he thought they should reschedule. He informed her that dinner was almost ready and they only lived minutes apart and he would see her soon. It took her a few minutes to translate the idea that he cooked and that would mean they would be at his house and if they were at his house, would she still stand by her new declarations about refraining from physical contact? Her core need to please her libido did not provide any confrontation on the subject. Besides, she can't recall ever having any Persian cuisine and she really liked the idea that he cooked.

She assumed that he must be doing his best to impress her. She considered what his age might be next to hers and reasoned that she must be careful not to lead him on but dressed her best none the less. He picked her up in a classic Lexus and he was dressed well too; complete with a youthful leather jacket. A shockwave went through her when she opened the car door and saw his features again. He was striking, indeed. He had an amazing smile and incredible dark eyes that pierced her when he would look at her. He smelled of mouth wash and cologne. She was glad. She adored the men who knew how to take care of themselves.

He explained that they were in his father's car; that his parents don't drive but he takes them on many errands. He mentioned the immigration office, social services offices and things like that. Both of his parents were still alive and able and lived in a house on their own. Stella thought this too was reminiscent of Ron's needy parents and how he always used them as an excuse for his unavailability. Time would only tell if this man would be doing the same. The two teased each other all the way to Raj's house. He showered her with compliments that fed her ego and allowed her to relax. He played with her hair and at stop lights look intently in her eyes and gripped the steering wheel tighter as if restraining himself from her with all his might.

Once there, after stepping from the garage, where a large, Iranian flag was hanging on the back wall, they noticed the almost full moon lingering right above his house. He turned, like a child, and held out both hands in the direction of the sky with the biggest, most endearing grin spread across his lips and announced,

"I give you the moon!"

Stella returned the beaming smile and responded quickly,

"Wow, the moon? And that is to start? Impressive." She playfully rebutted.

His home was unique; orderly, organized and ornate. The atmosphere was filled with music. He had set out candles all along the blonde, wooden floors in the living room. He said that he had wanted her to walk into the house with the den lit but that he was worried he might set a fire leaving candles burning alone. The logic placed his guest at ease and he offered her a seat on one of his two matching sofas. He sat down quite close to her and boldly slid his arm around her shoulders. She did not mind and rather felt quite comfortable with, in a familiar way.

Stella asks him about the painting above the fire place. It is the face of a woman painted all in black with a blood red background. He begins to tell her,

"That is Farah..."

He then pauses and waits for her reaction. In his home country of Iran, copies of this portrait are seen most in regions where Shi'a Islamic Extremists gather. It is an unmistakable symbol with dark connotations; but has also become fashionable for interior design, simply because it's size and bold colors. In that moment, it became clear to him that she knew nothing about Iran. Feeling as if an explanation of the picture might dampen the mood, he settles on a generic response,

"She was one of my lovers. She painted a self-portrait for me."

"I like it." Stella offers hesitantly.

Raj takes advantage of the awkward, silent moment to lean in and plant a kiss on Stella. Although the touch of his soft and perfect pucker was pleasing, she shimmied out from under his arm and asked if it would be alright if they could eat. She knew how painfully weak she was against pheromones and this man had her on a true overdrive already. This was her first and only attempt at resistance.

"Who is this girl? Raj says out loud.

They make their way into the kitchen and he attempts to recover from her surprise interruption of his seduction.

"Who is this girl" He repeats, "that asks for dinner in the middle of a kiss?"

Stella tries to brush off the jarring transition with enthusiasm.

"I am just interested in this Persian dish you've been raving about." She says and he compliments her on her strength of resistance and assures that he will shatter it.

He goes about stirring a pot on the stove and hurries around the kitchen preparing a delicious, Middle Eastern sandwich. He asks if she will assist in chopping some basil. She does what he asks and while she is working he leaves the kitchen and returns a few minutes later having changed from his pants into what she only assumed was a Middle Eastern wrap around his waist and an animal's look in his eyes. He was fully covered until he whipped his hips revealing the largest erection she had ever seen in her life.

This drew out a gasp from her and now he was sure he had spiked her interest. As she stood at the sink, she grappled with her desires. Licking her lips at his superior size, she turned her back to him to hide her weakening will. In an innocent attempt to distract him from her struggle, she swayed her hips at him knowing what this might imply. She didn't hold back because she was sure he would ask permission to come closer.

In the blink of an eye he was behind her; his hands pulling her hips to him, and he grinded his erection on her backside delivering conformation of his sheer size. It was this gesture that allowed her to abandon her resistance. She had been around and knew that his equipment was quite rare. After only a few seconds of indulgence of this dance, she peeled away again and reminded him of dinner. He agreed and they cooled off long enough to eat.

During dinner they spoke about past experiences and about the things they liked and disliked. They agreed to keep their relationship physical but Stella shut him down on the topic of anal sex. She had recently suffered a traumatic event in which she was with a guy she really liked and he ripped into her backside with great force and speed. She was in pain for days after and did not want to do that again.

After dinner they sat on the blanket he had spread on the floor. They were surrounded by lit candles and he poured them each another drink. He offered her some pot from a local dispensary and she was relieved he had. She was always able to hold her liquor better with the help of the medicinal plant. Once they were relaxed and comfortable, they quickly returned to the euphoria of their chemistry. He took his time but remained quite dominant.

Without restraint, he began tracing her entire body with his fingertips. Every part of Stella's skin stood covered in goose bumps as her eyes became drowsy with enjoyment. Raj pulled her to him;

29

kissing her. He then, stroked her hair from her face to gaze into her eyes. He told her she was a very beautiful woman and he was feeling very lucky to be in her presence this evening. She thanked him and took the opportunity to inquire about his age.

He stopped a moment and moved away from her. After a pause, he answered,

"I prefer to tell you when our date is over. I don't want you to have any preconceptions about me based on a number. Let me show you an amazing time and I assure you, you will not even care. Would that be alright with you?" He suggested.

Stella thought this was fair. She was already having an amazing time. He stood over her and held out his hand. She took his assistance standing up and he wrapped his right arm around her waist and took her by the hand with his left. He moved close to her as they began to dance in the middle of the floor to the music that filled the house. Again, he kissed her lips and she tenderly cupped his cheek with her hand. He was a good kisser and this drove Stella wild.

He slipped his fingers inside her dress at the buttons and opened them all with ease. She returned the favor, removing his shirt, leaving him in only his revealing wrap. They danced, kissed and caressed one another some more until, eventually, they stood, dancing naked. He offered her a seat on the couch where they continued exploring one another. He treated her curves like precious candy as he continued to move in closer. He embraced her tightly then, pulled her back to the floor and they followed their desires to the peak of anticipation.

When he finally slid into her, they both let out expressions of true ecstasy. He was so big in size and being aware of this, was gentle with her. She had never experienced, while engaged in amazing intercourse, her sight leaving her when the sensations became too great.

"I can't see, I can't see." She panted.

This ability he had to affect her senses turned him on even more. As she lay on the blanket, he continued to gently and in a slow rhythm, slide in and out of her. He was very vocal as they engaged in intense passion. He would rumble in her ear about how soft she was, how nice she smelled and how amazing she felt. Then he said as he rapidly pulled out of her and gave her his amazing smile,

"I want to try something. Can you do me a favor? Don't cum until I tell you to."

His excited eyes waited with anticipation at this request. It didn't take long for her to agree as she normally struggled to reach climax anyway. All of the men she had previously been with had left her responsible for her own apex when they were unable to crack the code. She knew very well how to take care of this but it required a certain concentration. His request would free her from this responsibility that most men rush. She loved the idea and he was such an entertaining lover he made it seem like a game. It also allowed for short bursts of wild, hard fucking until the build of a climax began to appear and then they would peel apart or sometimes push apart. They would drink, smoke, talk, laugh and dance in between fucking.

The separations built intense sensations that enhanced the pleasure when he would re-enter her. As she had her mouth on him, she was stricken with a familiar metallic taste. Embarrassed, she excused herself and closed herself in the bathroom to confirm her concern. When she returned to him, she admitted she had begun bleeding. To her surprise, he displayed a bit of giddiness and suggested to her that she let him take pictures of the mess. Stella refused to bring a camera into her sex life and spent some time arguing against the idea. Finally, he convinced her that he would not include her face in it and that he would look at them with her and they would delete them together. Eventually, Stella's need to please overruled her own objections and she held her ass in the air while Raj snapped two or three shots.

After they exhausted any entertainment the photos offered, Raj deleted the pictures and invited Stella to the shower. They seductively soaped one another up and he commented on her prickly pussy. She had shaved but he was into baldies. He asked if he could shave her and she agreed. He was slow and tender-handed and made her feel as if he were more familiar with the female shape than she was. He slowly drug the blade across her lips and her thoughts went to the only other time she allowed a man to groom her. It had been her

31

ex-husband while they were still dating and he was a bumbling idiot who accidentally cut her while she allowed him to shave her.

When he was finished, he petted her smooth flower, turned her around and instructed her to grab the side of the bathtub. After he thoroughly washed her lady parts, he slipped his still erect cock back inside of her. He pumped fast and rough expelling an unbridled hollering from her. The louder she screamed, the harder he rammed her and the more intense his own grunting would become until they were both shouting with pleasure,

"Yes! Yes! Oh, Yes!"

He pulled out of her again, leaving her weak and drooling as she still clung to the side of the bathtub. Because they were in the shower, she did not notice the tears streaming down her cheeks. She was gelatin. They dried off and just as soon as they were back in the living room he urged her to put her knees on the couch. When she did, she was pushed over, ass up and he dove into her again. She shouted with pleasure, her face buried into the pillows and their fuck fest continued. He asks her to get on top of him. She does reluctantly, for this position typically encouraged her climax.

She was only able to allow him to remain inside of her for moments at a time. Her struggle to subside her climax began to arouse Raj in a way that drew out a devious laughter from him. Once he believed she's had enough, he permitted her to climax. When she did, the intensity extracted loud panting and wild screaming and this combination sent Raj into a wild frenzy. His voice started low and followed the rhythm of Stella's panting,

"Yes, yes, yessss!"

He encouraged her as she rode him with a crescendo in her pace. The faster she moved, the more he shouted,

"Yes! Yes! Yes!!"

Faster and faster; louder and louder their voices both grew until they were both hollering,

"Yeeessss!"

An act that filled Raj with such excitement that he climaxed too.

They lay collapsed and tangled on the floor; sweaty and breathing heavily. Raj reached for his phone to check the time. It was two in the morning. This meant they had been fucking for four hours. They complimented one another over and over and he invited her back into the shower and asked her to help clean up and spoke of his need to keep things tidy. She finally decided it was time to know his age and boldly questioned,

"I am 60." He replied while Stella's jaw hit the floor and her head started shaking in doubt.

She dressed and after they kissed he said,

"I don't usually kiss my lovers."

She wondered if this was some sort of prelude to any follow up encounters. Then, they finished dressing and Raj took Stella home.

CHAPTER V

Swing

The next morning, Stella awoke with an enormous smile. Memories of the night flooded her, accompanied with shivers and lingering sensations. She was driven to immediately masturbate. The sounds of his satisfaction were ringing in her ears and she would be stricken by these feelings all day. Over and over, in her mind, highlights of last night's escapade bounced in her thoughts as she moved about her day, ever so slowly. Raj was a big man and she was feeling the truth of that today too.

Around 9am she received a text message with nothing more than a picture of a bouquet of pink and red rows of roses laid on a flat surface. No caption, no follow up text, just the flowers. This was confusing to Stella. He obviously wasn't shy. Maybe he was busy, she thought, and that was his way of fitting her in. Trying to provoke him, she replied,

"I see I've left you speechless."

But he did not take the bait. It would be a few more days before she would hear from him again. The complete silence that followed the splash of virtual roses chilled Stella's core. Something about the two dimensional gesture didn't sit well with her. When she finally did hear from him, he called rather than text. He proceeded to tell her he was leaving soon for Iran; a trip he goes on once or twice a year, for about a month at a time. This devastates Stella but she does not react.

Deep down she begins to feel like this had all been a set up. She had been romanced, de-pantsed and not given a second chance. Everything inside her was telling her it would be the last time she heard from him. She concluded that he probably didn't even live in that house and he likely rented it for days at a time while he was in the country and now he would be going home. Stella's heart stung already, "why?" She wanted to know. Why did he have to be the very best lover she had ever had?

Just as usual, Stella was agreeable and non- confrontational. She wanted to become angry and accuse him of being a predator, of stealing her heart and skipping town but remembered their conversation about keeping things physical. The words she wanted to say to him were filled with far too much emotion to comply and so she did the only thing she could; let him go. When they said their goodbyes, she truly believed he was leaving for good. Bidding him a safe and fun excursion was a forced act of repetition. This was it; Stella's big, predictable crash and burn. Like with Adam, he would capture her spirit and take it with him. Only, she would not be able to visit Iran to reclaim it.

For days after Raj left, Stella allowed herself to slovenly eat her feelings. Anything sweet or savory was subject to her consumption. The entire year, so far, had been spent working out to tone up and trim down. Knowing the reverse effects this allowance would produce, she indulged, none the less, because it was a life-long defense mechanism for her to pack on pounds to cover up her sexiness that appeared to only appeal to mean, spirit stealing men. When she was heavier, they didn't pay attention and if she's not considered, no one can steal anything from her.

She sat in front of the television for hours and became absorbed in the Alpha waves it produced. She was subject to tears anytime a commercial attempted to play a person's heart strings. She smoked an obscene amount of pot which only enhanced her ability to continue eating.

"What is wrong with me?"

She thought and questioned why she always ended up in that situation. Why this time does it have to be with the world's most magnificent lover? Why did she cave and sleep with him in the first place? That's why! No one can take her seriously because she doesn't know how to say "no."

This self-destruction went on for a full week before Stella decided enough was enough. She hadn't done anything productive since Raj left and this was not the kind of woman she wanted to be; taking to her bed in tears over a man. Turning her focus back to building her business, she went about reviewing and making changes to the website. This creative outlet was just what was needed to refocus Stella's mind and to help keep her life together. Her encounter with Raj had distracted her from the fact that she was only months away from needing a new place to live. Her sub-lease contract would be expiring and she wasn't sure she could lease another place with the way the timing was lining up again.

The contract at the country club was also coming to an end and she was terrified to know whether or not her new business would show income enough for the first few months. This evidence would be needed as proof of income in order to lease a new place. Her life in Santa Monica seemed to point to a vortex of struggle and if she let down her guard even once, she could be on her way out and headed to her sister's house. To cope with these realities, Stella returned to The Ruby Rabbit where she was never disappointed. She was doted on one way or another there.

Recalling the wise words of her good friend,

"The only way to get over a man is to get under another one."

Stella knew The Ruby Rabbit was the place for this. That night she received proposals of all sorts but she remained picky. Eventually she came across a Norwegian with a sizable package. The two headed to the cabanas that provide semi-privacy beds and she conducted a vigilant attempt to recreate the connection she experienced with Raj. This young man was handsome, blonde, built with lean muscle, not a flaw on his body and a decent sized dick. But no matter how hard and fast he pounded on her, there was nothing there. It was not enjoyable. She could only think of Raj.

There was an African American male standing outside the cabana licking his lips as he enjoyed the voyeurism the semi-privacy cabana allowed him. His erection confirmed he had been enjoying watching Stella take the Norwegian's generous endowment. With no thought or discussion, she invited the voyeur to join them. Barely even taking a glimpse at his face, she turned her back to him and positioned herself on all fours. No talking, no kissing, no foreplay; just an immediate invitation to fuck. The voyeur did not want to blow this rare opportunity. He inserted his inadequate penis into Stella. He took her by the hips and began slapping his own hips against her ass in a sloppy attempt to appear better at fucking than he actually was.

Who was he trying to kid, she thought. This was a smaller dick's way of "peacocking" knowing he isn't truly getting the job done. She went along with the charade for a minute and then out of pure disgust, made him stop. Stella suddenly began to question what it was that she was even doing. She kicked them both out of the cabana and then left the club to go home.

The next day while roaming the bookstore for some peace, quiet and a latte, she received a phone call from an unknown number. As usual, she did not answer it. The caller left a voicemail and she listened to it almost immediately. It was Raj. He said he was calling from Iran, that he was thinking of her and he had been shopping and couldn't resist bringing her a gift. He said that he would try to call again and extended his uniform pleasantries. She was blown away. All at once she felt excitement, guilt, anticipation and above all, though unsure why, fear.

With her new romance seemingly back on track, Stella again turned her focus back to her new business. Within the week she completed the changes to her website and received her business cards and menus. She spent hours at the county office to obtain her business license and tried not to complain about how tedious the waiting became. She was so excited she called everyone she knew to tell them about her new food cart, yet, stayed in to celebrate alone.

Once the silence set in from the completion of these goals, she found her thoughts drifting toward Raj. Since they spoke, her interest had been rejuvenated. Knowing that she was also on his mind would bring her far enough out of her funk to begin taking care of herself again.

CHAPTER VI

Oh! Wolfie!!

Inside the Hosseiniyeh Ershad in Tehran, the same building that housed meetings before the 1979 revolution, the evening sun poured bright beams of light through the windows. On the far wall hung a copy of the black and red image of Farah Pahlavi. The men seated in the rows of finished wooden pews, inside the beautifully tile-decorated building, focus on the message being delivered from a man at a podium. He begins with the typical, introductory praises and gratitude for Allah as if it were a code of conduct he was following. After the usual introduction, the man speaks in Farsi[4] with great intensity.

"Gentlemen I urge you to act as Allah would have you act. There is a great evil in the world today and it is our business, no, our duty to find a way to put an end to it. Along with the many other reasons we do not want to take part in the West's devious way of life."

The men could not have prepared for what they were about to see.

"Death to America!" The speaker shouted and the men hollered in echo.

---

[4] *Persian Language*

The list of offenses that resulted in death displayed on the screen.

"The people are not to be blamed; they are in fact, victims themselves but they have no minds and are subject to carry out the most evil of deeds. This could be against your brother or sister or mother or all of them. Imagine waking up tomorrow without them. We must intercept. Any man that can be controlled is expendable, any woman that can be controlled should also be put to death for they are no longer of God, they have become like beasts."

The Shia-Islamic Speech went on for quite some time. Raj turned down his television as roaring laughter ensued at the research of "stupid Americans." The program was becoming tiresome to him while the layers of propaganda were piled on. Soon, a slide show projected American men and women involved in crimes or outrageous acts. When the topic moved to the over-sexualized, female population, countless video clips of American women were shown in one compromising position or another. Blurred out close-ups of the women's vaginas were emphasized over and over.

"Look! None of these women are halal[5]! They are filthy!!" The man at the podium ranted.

This prompted Raj to get up and turn off the television completely. He thought about his new American lover who was also not halal. He had his own concerns about this but would not listen to someone shouting about it on T.V. Raj was well aware of the oversexed female American population. He had his own personal library of video evidence on his phone. Young, beautiful American women had all stepped inside his home, allowed him to fuck them and record the entire evening on his phone. He knew more than any of those men how littered the United States was with these mindless, directionless American women devoid of values or common sense.

Raj had been in the States long enough to understand that each of these women had several things in common. Most came from broken backgrounds and those who didn't were in some way neglected

---

[5] *Denoting or relating to preparation as described by Muslim law*

with just as much consequence. Their life long hunt for attention would forever distract them from the necessary solitude it takes to construct the type of mindset that would ultimately rescue them from such pathetic situations. The women he had been with should consider themselves lucky however he wasn't the type of guy to sell the material.

Another similarity these same types of women held was their constant survival mode. Their life remained in back to back chaos and this provided the perception to them that sex was a drug, an escape, a way to release some steam off of the everyday pressure cooker in which they would reside. And so, when in the heat of the moment, they are all too happy to strip off all inhibitions and take on the most carefree persona possible. To some, these women are considered "live bait."

"He's right, you know." Kohinoor said.

"My family wouldn't send me out into the world like that. They should have more respect for their bodies"

Kohinoor was a petite light skinned Iranian woman with shoulder length, silky black hair. She had only known Raj for a short time but he had seduced her effortlessly as he did all the others. Her will was no match for his serpent like charms. He moved with the grace of a beauty queen and reeled her in with an array of compliments that pretended to comfort the loneliness that her insecurities afforded her.

Raj started flipping through pictures of women in his phone for Kohinoor. She flinched when they came across the picture of Stella's bloody ass that he secretly had not deleted.

"Oh my God, what is that?!" she asked while terrified.

"Oh, darling, you know what this is; it is the procedure." He retorted.

"Who is that? She wondered.

"That is her; that is my new American lover."

"She LET you?" She questioned.

"How else will I bring her home to mâmân and bâbâ? He replied for effect with the embellished truth.

41

Kohinoor was shocked. He could almost see the moment her heart cracked.

"You care that much for this woman you just met?" Kohinoor persisted with anger in her tone.

"It is too soon to tell but she does have me intrigued." He answered.

A wave of jealousy washed over her as she pressed him.

"What's so intriguing about this stupid, American woman?"

Raj notices the unpleasant change in her attitude and glides right through it like water. He says to her,

"Oh, she is not stupid that is for sure. She's quite clever, in fact. Her mind is amazing in that she always has an extraordinary response. No matter what I say she is quick to direct my focus onto all things sexy. She is very different from Persian women."

Kohinoor suffers in silence as the praise for Stella droned on and on. Just as Raj started in on how she was so different that he would bet that when he returned to the States they would have a threesome.

Kohinoor replies, "Oh, she sounds terrific. This woman seems to arouse you from around the world. How will I compete?" She lashes at him beginning to feel somewhat disrespected, considering she was the only woman in the room.

"Maybe I should go?"

Kohinoor tests as she begins to gather her things. She knew how to demand her own focus and her threat awakens Raj from the Western fantasy back into his Middle Eastern reality. Kohinoor was there with him now and Raj would not let that change. He grabbed her arm in protest.

"You don't want to leave, lover." His heavy breath became even heavier and very methodical and audible as he rolled his eyes into his head. He closed them while he nuzzled her face and showed his teeth. His exaggerated volume drew her pattern of breathing in to match his and soon she was drunk on his pheromones. Kohinoor dropped her things and quickly undressed in front of him.

"Slow down, slow down." He begged.

"Slowly, no rush."

Kohinoor did not seem to hear Raj, or rather, she seemed to ignore his request.

"I am not your stupid American whore, Raj." Kohinoor charged.

Raj grandly raised his hand and boldly slapped her across the cheek so hard her head turned from the force. She held her hand to her burning red face. When her head finally straightens out, they are nose to nose as he hissed at her,

"She is not a stupid American woman, do you hear?"

Kohinoor becomes frightened and nods her head in a subordinate fashion.

"I am not sharing these things with you in order to arouse jealousy. I am sharing them because I want them to turn you on." He explains.

"I am not that kind of girl." She says softly.

"No, no, you're not are you, kitten?" He oozes as he begins his enchantment of her.

"You're a respectable, desirable Iranian woman and I should treat you with such esteem. Forgive me my love, my lust runs deep and you turn me on just the sight of you."

Raj caresses Kohinoor's body in a tenderly fashion. His fingers relax her well enough that she eventually and predictably presents her ready self to him by lying on her back. The physical side of Raj was the only thing present while his mind wandered back across the globe to Stella and her intriguing set of open boundaries. He imagined his evening with Stella as he closed his eyes and slipped inside Kohinoor and maintained the rhythm of a metronome. This is the way of life for most sexually repressed Persian women. Back and forth he pumped his hips to her deep, raspy, involuntary moaning.

He attempted to speed up his pace and was quickly corrected. He tried again with a slower incline to his speed using more audible breathing again as he had before. This time it paid off. Soon, Kohinoor was sweating and panting and thrusting her hips. This may have gone on for quite some time had he not indulged in his delight by growling,

"Oh, yeah, that's a good girl."

Her eyes pierced his as she stopped her movements all at once. Suddenly, Raj found himself fucking a motionless, angry woman.

"Oh, stop it. That is not funny."

He demanded but Kohinoor just lied there, still, looking into his eyes with contempt. He pulled out of her and rose to his knees. As Kohinoor attempted to get up and turned over, Raj grabbed her knee and pulled it out from under her causing her to belly flop onto the bed. Raj did a spread eagle, covering her entire body from limb to limb with his own. He then appealed to her feminine side as he kissed her shoulders and the back of her neck until she stopped her struggle. Testing her, Raj used his right hand to tease her with his cock. He slips back inside of her and took her with much force and speed and dominance. She doesn't make a sound and Raj repeats to her,

"Yea, you like that don't you? You want to know how I want to fuck my dirty American lover? Here! Here! This is how! Do you like it?"

She nods her head as he continues to gain speed. Excited that she is not protesting, he grabs a fist full of her hair and pulls her head back. She says to him,

"You needn't be so rough."

He bellows at her as he thrusts his hips, as if on cue, while he emphasizes the words of his choice,

"YOU LOVE IT, you bitch, you LOVE IT!"

Kohinoor mumbles under her breath,

"Stupid American sluts."

And when Raj heard this, he stood up, gathered her things and dismissed her from his house. She begged him not to make her leave but he had a switch, that when flipped, stood as stubborn and as cold hearted as they come. He would no longer look her in the face and he held his hand in the air for her to stop talking. He continued helping her put her items in a pile and then stared at her with irritation while she dressed. Silence fell over the house once he turned off the

44

music and as she leaned in to kiss him goodbye, he turned his head, rejecting her.

CHAPTER VII

The Sounds Lovers Make

Stella was excited that Raj was returning that day. He had given her the date when they spoke and had since left her another message of his arrival. When his flight landed, he wasted no time. Before he could even get off the plane he sent Stella a text:

"Just landed. See you soon."

Though she is thrilled, her caring instincts take over and she sends a message back:

"Raj! I am so anxious to see you but if you're exhausted we can reschedule."

Raj responds,

"See you soon." attached with a picture of an orange butterfly over blue rocks.

She thought this strange at first but then reasoned that they can't always be flowers. Then, Stella began to beam. She thought she must have made some impression on him to skip any sort of rest in lieu of a sexual escapade with her. Though she was only slightly uneasy about the reunion falling on the eve of Valentine's, she tried not to let that distract her. He told her he had come bearing gifts and so she felt inclined to put together her own sweet surprise.

As she readied that evening, she took special care to shave thoroughly in all areas for a smooth finish. Knowing now, his emphasis on cleanliness, she took great care in the shower to scrub every crease she had, including between her toes. After her shower she touched up the paint on her nails, lathered up her whole body with lotion and spent no less than an hour on her hair and makeup. The man had been on her mind since he left and the anticipation to see him again was almost unbelievable. No one had occupied her thoughts with such consistency since she had been released from the prison that Adam held on her mind.

Raj had been able to convince Stella that his urgency to see her was equally as pressing. He arrived to pick her up. The moment she saw him her tongue unwittingly ran across her teeth and the heat was on. He reacted in surprised delight. They simmered in the short car ride to his house. Each trying to over- emphasize with their eyes that they are ravenous with lust for one another. Entering his house, for the second time, was much the same as it was the first. Everything was neatly in place. He had lit the candles this time and started up the music right away. There was a fire in the fireplace and more candles on the table with a strange, feminine looking string of pearls draping the table. They both agree to take off the bottom half of their clothing, to get more comfortable.

Right away, they start rubbing on one another and kissing each other's bodies. Just as the intensity is building, he pulls away and says,

"Wait, I don't want to forget, I have a gift for you."

"So do I." She follows.

Her announcement surprises him and he shakes his head in disbelief as he disappears into a bedroom. While he is gone, she exits to the kitchen to retrieve an envelope from her purse. When they meet back in the living room she is sitting on the couch in front of the fire. He first gives her a bag of shelled nuts. The bag is written in Farsi leaving her unaware of what kind they are.

"They are pistachio nuts." He tells her then reaches for his other gift to her.

It is a wrap, closely modeled after the one he wore when he seduced her last month. It was a soft, peach colored cloth with knotted tassels on each end and printed in Persian, was what Raj described as a poem.

"One day I will translate the entire poem for you
but today I will tell you that the first word of this poem says "Love.""

Stella adored his style of romance and yet still, inside, remained on such high alert. There was just something about Raj but she didn't know what, so, she tried to let the feeling roll off her shoulders. She praised and praised the beauty and thoughtfulness of the gift he brought and made her advance to return the gesture. He opened the flap and read the silly, suggestive, humorous card he had pulled from the red envelope. The punchline, unfortunately, was lost in translation. Then he removed the other item from the envelope. It took him only seconds to recall their first encounter at the grocery store as he searched for a packet of Hollandaise mix, which he now held in his hand.

This tickled Raj with delight and laughter and he kissed her face and referred to her as,

"You darling woman!"

It fascinated him that her memory and charm were so polished. She knew just how to be a lover. Raj told Stella that he knew she was different. He told her that he had bragged to his Persian lover about her and that he tried to explain their differences to her but that she hadn't understood.

"How am I so different, do you think? Stella wanted to know.

"Persian women aren't sensual like you. They're sexual but in a different way. They don't play like you. They don't think like you."

In an act that caused Stella to think her gift resulted in his immediate arousal, he invited her to the shower with him where he, much like before, lathered her up and went about foreplay in the steaming, porcelain tiled bathroom. He then slid his fingers between the lips of her vagina and an expression of excitement came over him to learn that her shaving had been thorough.

"So smooth! I like! Look at the lover, so disciplined; I say smooth and she makes it smooth for me. Oh, she is so good."

He encouraged her and she began to embrace her sensuality. She wanted this man and could hardly wait to have him again. She stooped down on one knee and quickly kissed his hard cock. It was so warm and so clean that she could not resist licking it a little like a lollipop and eventually put her whole mouth down on top of it. He turned off the water as they remained there dripping wet, while Stella was busy creating a thick coat shine on Raj's Persian package.

Soon they are on the living room floor and wildly going at it. The satisfaction and pleasure when their bodies joined was overwhelming for Stella. They embraced and closed their eyes in ecstasy and savored the moment. Progressively, she wound up on her knees and Raj was riding her from behind. The sensations were unlike any she had ever felt or had known. Letting go of her whole mind may have proved to be a mistake, as she involuntarily had a slip of the tongue and panted,

"I love you!"

Right away Stella became aware of her lapses linguae and slowly turned her head toward his face to see if there had been any reaction. Raj had not seemed to notice and for a time Stella hid her face in the blanket below. She was astounded. That had never happened to her before in her life. Even to the man she had married had she only ever offered a voluntary confirmation of devotion. She was not able to recall a single time in her life that words flew out of her mouth without them ever having crossed her mind, so that she had a chance to stop them.

This phenomenon happened one other time when they were together, which was quite often.

One night he messaged her spontaneously and asked if she could go for a ride. To be clever she responded,

"A car ride, a joy ride, a ride on a white horse?"

He seemed to revel in her word play and responded in kind.

"A joy ride on a dark horse."

He showed up in a brand new Mercedes. Intrigued, she slipped into the car and began her natural inquisition. He gave her a cup with whiskey and cola as well as an energy shot. She drank half the energy shot, while Raj downed his. Stella also pretended to take large gulps of her whiskey drink but was truly only putting the liquid to her lips to provide the false pretense that she had been drinking all along.

They arrived at a bathhouse in the mountains and he was charming, considerate and playful the entire time; that is, until Raj had a spell come over him. He began to have feelings of dizziness and a sour stomach. Stella knew it was the alcohol mixed with the heat of the sauna. She opened the door while he lied down. Raj thought some food might help him but didn't know where to find any.

Suddenly, Stella remembered she had half a package of mini donuts in her purse from an earlier, naughty, craving she had given into. The very fact that she had donuts in her purse was shameful to Stella but Raj was suffering and so she looked beyond her embarrassment and offered him the pastry. He enthusiastically accepted her offer and when she tried to hand it to him, he barked at her,

"Just put it in my mouth!"

Part of Stella wanted to interrupt,

"Oh, no you didn't!"

Instead, she graciously looked past this strange personality trait because she knew he was hurting and like a humble servant, placed a donut in Raj's mouth. This miraculously revived him and he repeated, in a humorous, way as if in shock each time, "Donut!"

He simultaneously extended his thanks for her rescue and kindness.

The two took part in regular meetings for wild and uninhibited sex. Raj's curiosity for voyeurism became increasingly apparent. First, it was about arranging the mirrors in the house in just the right position. This was sexy but time consuming. Then, she found herself arguing about the use of his video camera on his phone. She put up a hefty fight but then agreed to allow this with the provision that they watch them together after and they also delete them together.

On a sunny Sunday afternoon Stella propositioned Raj by text.

"I was hoping you had some time for me to stop
by."

"What time?" He asked.

"Around two"

"See you then." She teased,

"Please be dressed in your Sunday best."

"Smiles" He texted back

At two o'clock, Stella arrived at Raj's house dressed in a conservative skirt and top with her hair tight in a French twist and a Bible in her arm. When he answered the door she began a typical Christian door-to-door witness speech in a southern accent. He smiled emphatically and invited her in. They exchanged dirty dialogue while she pretended her daddy was the pastor of her church. He pretended to know about her naughty habits and threatened to tell on her about her misbehavior unless she did what she was told.

He told her to suck his cock. He told her to lick his ass. He told her to suck on his balls, hard. He told her to bend over. As she stood in the middle of the floor, she bent over and grabbed her ankles. He roughly spanked her a few times before flipping her skirt up over her back to reveal that she wasn't wearing any panties. She was prepared for a ramming but instead received a soft lapping of his perfectly, cool, supple tongue on her soaking wet, ever smooth, ivory pussy.

Eventually Raj takes the opportunity to slide his large, male organ inside of Stella's beautifully presented lady flower. He takes hold of her hips in order to balance them both in the exotic position. First, he moved slowly, then, switched quickly to pumping her fast until he would have to stop to maintain his erection. Again, slow then fast. He continued this pattern for five or six cycles until he let out a holler of frustration as he walked away,

"Aaaahhhhhh! I want to cum but I can't, I have a date in a little while and if I cum now, I won't be able to later." He announced.

Stella's head was pointed to the ground and so her face was hidden from Raj while a devious grin spread across it. Stella liked the idea that she would be intercepting some other, poor woman's night. She quickly put reverse psychology into action.

51

"Oh, OK. I understand. We can finish this another time."

She offered as she began gathering her things. Raj rushed to her.

"Don't go yet, you naughty girl." He played while groping her all over.

"I have to go or my dad will start to get suspicious." She continued in her role playing character.

"You know I'm going to tell your daddy what you've been up to unless you do what I say, right?" He joined.

"Oh, please don't tell on me, sir. I did what you wanted, what else do you want?" She plead.

"I want you to turn around and bend over." He suggested.

"Well, um, I would but I really must be going. I don't want to get in trouble."

"But I am not finished and don't forget I can get you into just as much trouble."

"I'm sorry I'll try to stop by another time. It was nice meeting you."

Stella started for the door. Raj was highly aroused by her insubordination and fiercely grabbed her arm and snatched her back toward him. He looked at her with anger and domination then spun her around and pushed her head back toward the ground into the same position she was in moments before. Grunting with authority, he yanked her skirt to the floor and slapped her ass several times. As quickly as he could, he unbuckled his belt again and let his pants drop.

Offering no hesitation, Raj plunged back into Stella. He leaned forward, wrapped his arms around Stella's upper torso and drilled at her backside without reservation of any sort. Shouts of pleasure escaped them both over the backdrop of silence. Not wanting to refrain any longer, Raj pulled out of Stella to show her his climax. At this, Stella, smiled with satisfaction knowing that whoever he would be with later was out of luck tonight, now that she got the best of him today.

The morning after this fantasy, Raj sent an unusual text.

"And the Academy Award goes to Stella Pilot for her role as the Shy Bible Girl in "The Sound Lovers Make."

She loved that he poked fun at their role play and these words convinced her that he adore her.

This would not be the best of them. Another time they took part in an all-night escapade together, Raj hung a long sash of fabric from the wall in front of the couch. They took turns tying one another up in erotic positions and while swimming in the glory of the moment, Stella shouted,

"This is the Cirque du Soliel of sex!!"

He laughed from the core of his belly at the beauty and accuracy of her observation. He truly enjoyed her ability to make such plays on words. She was in trouble though. Their harmony had her heart opening up to Raj. Would she be able to continue protecting herself?

CHAPTER VIII

Fringe

Stella's birthday was set to fall on a Saturday. Having mentioned this occasion a few times already to Raj and not receiving an invitation to celebrate, Stella planned to go play at The Ruby Rabbit on her own. The Ruby Rabbit was having a theme party and the occasion was Easter. Stella's tradition when attending theme parties was to dress outside the usual ideas for costumes. She would include only use a trace of the theme in order to stand out. For Valentine's Day when everyone was in formal wear, she arrived in a black and red apron... only. For the winter black and white ball she dressed in Tom Cruise's infamous large, white button down with white socks and black sunglasses. For St. Patrick's Day, she wore gold pajamas, gold high heels and covered her whole body in gold glitter to become a pot of gold. This time was no different; she dressed in a pink and black 20's flapper dress and wore neon, glowing pink bunny ears to remain on the edge of the theme.

While piecing together her costume, she received a text from Raj inquiring about her afternoon. Ecstatic but not wanting to act too eager, she waited about an hour before responding. He asked if she was busy that afternoon and she told him she was working on something.

"What?" He requested.

"My costume; I'm going to a theme party tonight."

"I see." He replied.

"Might you have some time this afternoon to play?"

"I'll see if I can fit you in. I'm pretty busy today."

These words fooled neither of them. He knew as well as she did that heaven and earth could be moved if it meant they could get together and become lost in ecstasy.

"If you are busy, I understand but please do your best."

An hour went by and she messaged Raj that she could swing by for a little bit at four.

"Wonderful. We will enjoy an afternoon delight." He teased.

She knew that it would be of extraordinary delight. This was the best gift, in her opinion. He clearly did not recall it was her birthday but the coincidence that he rung for her on that day offered her satisfaction not withholding. Feeling as if she had conquered her birthday's desire, she second guessed if she would even attend the party at The Ruby Rabbit. After all, Raj is what she truly wanted. Secretly, Raj is what she truly wanted all the time. She didn't care anymore about conquering other men. She believed it wasn't ever going to be better than it was with Raj.

She recalls the countless random affairs in which she took part; none of which were because she desired them. Since she had met Raj, all the affairs were simply to maintain the notion that Raj did not want her heart. If Raj had said to her at any point that he wanted to become serious about her, she was willing, ready and able to drop all of her philandering, which in itself had become burdensome. She knew it wouldn't be different at all either because she found her thoughts with Raj even as she was with other men.

For example, one cold, self-protecting night, Stella had been out with a man she originally met at The Ruby Rabbit but who she also continued to see privately. Stella and this man were catching their breath, after their own high chemistry sex, in his downtown apartment. The man had fallen asleep and Stella was lying next to him wondering how long she should stay before she went home. Stella never stayed the night with any men. Not even Raj. It was a rule of hers, in order to maintain a clear understanding of the dynamics she was involved in. As she pondered, she heard her phone buzz with a text message notice from the next room.

She slipped out of bed to check her phone and saw that it was Raj. A devious smile fell over her face and she responded to her favorite lover. Raj asked her what she was doing.

"I am in bed." She replied.

"Get dressed and come over." He suggested.

"OK." She agreed and she went about gathering her things from the man's apartment while he slept soundly in his bed; comfortably resting without a clue of the sexual deviance Stella was about to commit. She kissed his forehead and as he opened his eyes, she said,

"I cannot stay."

He gestured with his hand to condone her departure, too stricken with sleep to rise and become aware. She was safely outside of the apartment when the same devilish smile drifted across her face. She would wear this same smile all the way to Raj's house. When he let her in, he noticed her fresh makeup and evening attire.

"I don't believe you were just in bed." He observed.

Stella chuckled and was so pleased with herself to retort to Raj - and hope it stung a little -

"I didn't say I was in MY bed."

Raj's eyes became wide with surprise as Stella's giggle built into a belting laughter. The smile never left Raj's face. He too enjoyed this situation.

"You were on a date?" He asked.

Stella nodded to confirm. Raj's body stood suddenly with enormous confidence. He was rocking side to side on his feet in a very masculine way. He flicked his hands in much the same fashion as The Fonze from *Happy Days* would before combing his hair. A big toothy grin crossed his face and he pressed again.

"So, you're saying, *I stole* you from another man's bed?"

Stella nodded again. Raj exploded with delight and took Stella in his arms as if what she had done was an amazing gift.

When Stella arrived at four o'clock on the afternoon of her birthday, Raj did not have any blankets or candles or pillows arranged on the floor. Instead, they went straight into his bedroom. This was extreme for Stella's thoughts. She couldn't have been more pleased to share his sheets. Plus, there were large, sliding glass mirrors on his closet which made for easy pleasing of Raj's voyeurism. Two hours passed quickly and they had to peel themselves apart, having both made individual plans for the evening. They agreed to part ways, attend these events and each hunt for a woman to join them when they later reconvened back at his house.

Stella had come to accept that since Raj had forgotten her birthday, she wouldn't be seeing him at all. Instead, she would end up spending tons of time with the man she adored making it special for her. She did mention the occasion to him again and he made no comment on it following. They parted, Stella went home to dress and did, in fact, look devastatingly amazing and the neon bunny ears were a crown of beauty. Her pink and black 20's flapper dress stood out among the obvious costumes. The black fringe swished back and forth as she moved around the club where she had come to be known as a regular. Like most nights when Stella walked in, she turned many heads. She carried with her a box of candies to share which made for a great ice breaker. It also made her stand out which was very important to Stella.

She sauntered around the bar and found a seat where she could flirt with the cute bartender and would order two drinks; downing the first and taking advantage of her immediate buzz to walk around the club and sip on the other. On this night, she did an amazing amount of teasing. Knowing she had an after party to attend, she wasn't on the hunt so much for a man as she was for a woman. She attempted a few times to seduce a few women away from the men they were on dates with to join her and her Persian Lover in a night of erotic pleasure that she believed they would all remember for the rest of their lives.

57

Unfortunately, these women did not want to leave the safety of the club. This did not turn out to be a disappointment, however, as Raj was quite skilled at seduction himself and soon sent Stella a picture of a beautiful pair of candle lit breasts with an invitation to join them. Too drunk to leave right away, Stella made a round of the club to show off the present that awaited her as soon as she chose to claim it. Many hugs and kisses and birthday spankings were offered to her on the way out. This place made her feel like a celebrity. Yet, she was pleased as punch to be leaving if it meant heading to Raj's.

She arrived at Raj's to find him and his friend, Banu, fully naked and draped in the precise setting she was once adorned with; blankets, pillows, candles, candies, the works. The music was so loud they shouted their introductions and Raj offered Stella a drink. He automatically requested approval from Banu.

"What do you think?"

Banu responded, "She is good, very beautiful."

Without even removing her pink and black dress, he pressed Stella's shoulders to encourage her to her knees and stuck his dick in her unsuspecting mouth. Not in need of much chit chat, Stella flipped on her motor and began to suck with emphasis on Raj. The three conducted the evening much like Stella and Raj did when they were alone. Sessions of kissing, licking, sucking and fucking were broken with drinks or smoking a little pot and small talk. Banu was a cigarette smoker and Raj joined her in the kitchen with his tobacco pen. During this, Stella situated herself on her knees to take turns licking his and her ass. She persuaded them that tobacco wasn't necessary as they both put out their cigarettes to return to the orgy.

Suddenly, a wave of nausea washed over Stella. She knew this feeling too well and so quickly decided to gather her things and make a silent exit. She was drunk. At The Ruby Rabbit she drank more than usual and people were buying her random shots all night for her birthday. Since arriving at Raj's, she had had even more alcohol. She snuck into the bathroom to dress. Raj followed her and begged to know what was wrong.

"I am too drunk, I'm not feeling well, I'm sorry, I have to go." She explained.

"No!" He insisted.

"You cannot leave. Just breathe, maybe it will pass. Please try."

Stella agreed she would try but knew her body and knew also that once this feeling came over her, there was no going back.

"Is there anything I can do?" He tried.

"Leave, please!" She begged him; the thought of being sick in front of him was mortifying.

Raj obliged and left the bathroom. She slammed the door behind him and prepared herself over the porcelain toilet. Feeling it rise, she did everything in her power to hold it back. To her surprise, she succeeded but the relief that regurgitation typically provides was also absent. Eventually, feeling as if she had conquered the nausea, she dressed and left the bathroom. She came to say her goodbyes but Raj would not hear of it. He took Stella by the hand and led her to the bedroom where he slipped off her pink and black dress again and told her just to rest. This gesture was so wonderful of Raj, Stella thought.

He would come in the room intermittently to check on her. He soon came in to lay with her and while he was there, Banu dressed and left. Stella tried and tried to leave too but Raj continued to insist she lay in bed and rest. She begged him not to let her fall asleep and insisted that she had to go home. So, Raj set his alarm for every 30 minutes. All through the night she would try to get up to these alarms and each time was still too drunk. Then, Raj would grab her hand as he lay next to her, still and sleeping, and she just couldn't leave the pleasure of this painful drunken sleep in which he held her hand.

Finally, at 5am she was sober enough to dress and sneak out. By this hour, Raj was too asleep to try and stop her. She went home, texted him her gratitude for his kindness, dropped her pink and black dress to the floor and went to bed. Just before passing out, she said to herself,

"Happy Birthday, Stella."

CHAPTER IX

Without Consent

Raj and Stella's encounters were countless after three months and they showed no signs of slowing. They would often sacrifice sleep for the unimaginable pleasure of fucking one another. Stella commented that she understood he was with other women and also knew that he probably felt the same intensity with them. He did not say anything right away but later confirmed to her that things were, in fact, not this way with other women. He wanted her to know at his exaggerated age that never in his life had he come across someone like her and that in a lifetime she shouldn't expect to find another that would match their chemistry.

Stella felt she had been most careful thinking about rejecting Raj again and again because he did not want her heart. But the intoxication of their physical encounters was too enticing for her to follow through. Once she had tried and was brought to tears. Raj interpreted this to mean she had feelings for another man. She loudly protested,

"No!"

As she buried her face in the blanket and sobbed. During her melt down she had wanted to shout,

"It's you! I have these feelings for you!"

But she knew from experience he would not respond in kind. She chose to allow the devastation to her heart in order to continue the exquisite intercourse her and Raj conducted in weekly. It was always extreme and unwavering satisfaction accompanied with the height of sensations and this became more and more addictive.

One night Stella arrived at Raj's and he presented her, upon entering, with a table full of liquors.

"Your choice!" He boasted.

She chose whiskey as usual when offered and he poured a healthy dose for her consumption. She eyeballed the glass with caution yet drank the entire thing. They had become accustomed to talking and snuggling soon after her arrival and Stella enjoyed this so much but the actions confused her into believing their relationship was something it was not. She was just so enamored with Raj and she wanted him to want her heart. Stella would come to be confused for a long time about what it is Raj really wanted.

As expected, the room was already set up with candles, blankets, sweets, pearls, pillows; the usual. He invited her to shower and she began to wonder why she bothered spending an hour in the shower at her own home before they met. He would just request that she take another so that he may be in charge of the thoroughness of the scrubbing. On this night, Raj asked Stella to,

"Turn around and grab ahold of the side of the bathtub; and don't look back, please."

Stella was resolved she would do just about anything for that gorgeous face. She didn't mind the extra doting. Suddenly, Raj inserted a douche wand into her and forced the vinegar mixture inside her. She was stunned and confused and scrambling to justify this. All at the same time she recalled how she had been enjoying the cleansing sessions before intercourse so that they could both relax feeling more confident that nothing about them would be offensive. Had she become offensive to Raj, she wondered? Should she be offended or does she just accept that these things are part of being a part of Raj's world?

It wasn't long before the process was over and Raj was on his knees with his face buried in Stella's backside. He was taking generous laps at her fresh as a daisy pussy and this was releasing the recently inflated tension the surprise douche had incited. For a time he continued to eat her in a way that made him appear ravenous for it. He grabbed her ass and squeezed so hard he left fingerprints in red that remained there as long as the sting of a spanking.

Back in the living room, Stella reached for one of his soft blankets. It was cold in the house after they showered. He was naked, almost stomping, as he waltzed towards the living room and announced,

"It is time."

"Time for what?" Stella wondered.

Boldly, he answers,

"It is time for you to be fucked in the ass."

"Ha ha." Stella forced. "No, not tonight, not me, I don't do that."

"Oh yes, darling, you will love it, trust me. I will be gentle, I promise." Raj attempted.

"No, no, I really don't think so." She insisted.

"Of course, we will see." He said and then moved in to place his usual spell on her; the one that made her weak in his arms.

Raj began to gently make love to Stella. He wooed and swooned at her and she was lost in his tricks in an instant. The way her body felt when they were connected was unlike anything she had ever known. Never had she lost track of so many senses at once; her sight, her intuitions, her perceptions of time, all escaped her for the total, physical envelopment that took place when he was inside of her. The feeling was so overwhelming she became completely engaged in the moment.

Raj stood up and left the room and as he did, instructed Stella to get into her favorite position. She loved taking it from behind so she turned onto her tummy and when he returned he was pleasantly surprised at her choice. He carefully angled the large mirror in front of them so they could both look on as they continued their lust filled work. Without foresight enough to know that Raj really was going to have his way with her tonight, she patiently waited for his return. Instead of the usual, glorious, sexual intercourse she visited frequently for, he used her position against her and began to slowly insert himself into her anus.

"No!"

She demanded as she tried to struggle beneath him. He pressed his hips just hard enough to paralyze her into submission. She felt a forced anal entry before and knew she did not want to feel it again. At this, she surrendered her fight. He held her by the neck and forced her to look into the mirror and watch as he continued to enter into the place he was not welcome. She started to show signs of pain and once the wiggling ensued, he would instruct her to be calm and "push" against him. This is the same sensation as having a bowel movement. Stella was humiliated.

In the reflection of the mirror, Raj seemed to have a different face. The noises he was making were different. It was as if he were all together a different person. She did not recognize this look of self-indulgent deviance. She was used to his kind and generous face. It did not match what she saw in the mirror. This man looked wicked, this man was frightening. Raj too could read the expressions on Stella's face. The more he furrowed his eyebrows at her, the more frightened she became and it read all over her face.

Never too fast, he maintained slow and methodical movements. He wanted her to enjoy it but the idea that she didn't turned him on just as much. He did not, however, take advantage of that and attempt to buck his hips in a way that would have torn her apart. Stella was relieved that it didn't last too long. He pulled out of her and went to grab some wet towels. He told her to stay where she was and that was fine with her because she was in so much pain from the anal entry.

Raj returned and Stella was still lying on her tummy. He gently patted her backside with the warm towels and then her entire groin area. He took advantage of her compromised positions to stick a few of his fingers back up inside her ass. One time he did this and she jumped because it felt like a pin prick. Raj's eyes became wide when she jumped and began to massage the very spot she thought she had felt the sharp poke. His attempt to calm her worked right away. She

63

desired him so that she trusted him far too much, or so she always thought.

Stella relaxed again and his massage continued. She felt like a queen. She had suffered for her lover and now he was delivering amazing gratitude. She was happy with the conclusions she was drawing as Raj again crammed his index and middle fingers into Stella's anus. This time she thought, it hardly felt like anything at all.

When he removed his fingers, he told her to be still, that she was bleeding. Stella believed this to be an exaggeration and was sure the blood was just from the tearing of her ass and didn't consider he meant much more blood than that. He instructed her to the bathroom where he had already started warming up the shower and the sink faucet was running full speed. He held a large amount of wet towels to clean her then told her to grab onto the sink. She does without question and he grabs at her inner labia. Stella then feels the sensation of a band aid that's being ripped from her vagina, only, wasn't wearing one.

"Ouch, what the hell are you doing?!" She shouts, feeling far more inebriated than she did only five minutes earlier.

"You are bleeding. Raj answered. "You have started your period. Check." He tells her.

Stella reached down and grabbed a handful of blood. She is mildly embarrassed that this has happened again. They look at each other and shrug and he motions her toward the shower. This was the obvious choice in such a situation. As they climb in, Raj complains,

"Oh, sweetheart, I expected a lot more screaming. That was a big dick."

She responds only with a shocked face that he would have the audacity to say such a thing. Meanwhile, inside, Stella is furious and satisfied knowing that her chosen silence during the unwanted anal sex was as displeasing to him as the act was to her. But now she was certain, this affair was over. She couldn't say "no," nor would he hear it. Either way, she was no longer safe if she wasn't in control.

CHAPTER X

Grooming

The next morning Stella slept in longer than usual. It was almost noon before she felt like she could even move. She was a mess. Her period had come on unusually strong. Also, the consequences of anal penetration were still punishing her. Stella was in a deepened pain. There were certain muscles she simply could not use.

"What the hell, Stella?" She said to herself while changing her feminine products. She was preparing for a long day in bed. She was so saddened and moved to tears as she had been the morning after her first unwanted anal entry experience. She truly felt betrayed by Raj. She knows she protested and remembered saying, "No." Now, she was in so much unbearable agony and how unfortunate for her this happened at the same time she started what was turning out to be the worst period of her life.

She wondered why things had gone in this direction. She knew he was very interested in the act but she was certain their discussions had included a solid, "No" on the subject. She was also devastated because now what had been so magical and eventful and the closest, she worried, she might ever come to a real life fantasy, had come to an end. Stella was in search of her own best and in her mind that did not include allowing someone to torture her. She hadn't been strong enough in the moment, again, to enforce her will over his and was genuinely distraught to know that this meant it was over between them.

For all the declarations Stella made about never speaking to him again, she often and in a way that was opposing to her declaration, checked her phone to see if there was a text message from him that she could ignore. It was so hot or cold with Raj when it came to a phone call the day after an intense evening. This time, Stella did not receive one. She was fine with that. It just allowed her to begin the process of letting him go that much sooner.

Stella's pain was great. She stayed in bed for three days and nursed her damaged undercarriage while also caring for her unbelievably heavy period. She was bleeding through pads even while using a tampon. It was so awful to deal with at the same time as the immense pain her bottom felt. She typically didn't have to deal with cramps either but this month her insides felt as if she had been through surgery. As she lied in bed, she began to think about the way she felt the day after unwanted anal penetration with the other mean man she had come across.

That had only been the act of forced entry, once and then the experience was done. She recalls herself screaming loudly enough to frighten him and he stopped immediately. With Raj, it was as if Stella didn't have the ability to say no and screaming hadn't seemed appropriate. As a result, she was now living the hurt from not only entry from a far more largely endowed man who forced his way in and out for quite some time but also living the hurt from a true broken heart. She simply couldn't believe it had happened again. Why? Why were men so interested in putting their dicks in her ass?

This cannot be happening again, she thought. She felt as if it weren't fair that such lightening had struck her twice. She wanted to know what the lesson was and possibly what the reason was that she was sentenced to repeat this pain; and on a much grander scale. Even though Stella had noticed uneasy feelings about Raj all along, these did not come to her mind right away.

When she finally emerged from her bed, three days later, she promptly hopped in the shower. She took her time letting the warm water fall over her but her mind remained on the other night. Over and over she played out the order of events and the disappointment she felt, was in herself, because her will was too weak against the urgings of her intuition. As she toweled off, she caught a glimpse of herself in the mirror. She reached for her vagina to get a better look at what she thought was a different shape than what she was used to. Her hand came back bloody with menstruation which ended the inspection at once.

"Wow!" She thought,

"Things look different when you shave bald all the time."

She considered just how much she had been shaving since she met Raj. An entire week went by before Raj reached out. She had spent the entire week thinking that they both knew it was over. She had already begun mourning her companion and their relationship as she had once known it. Stella tried to relieve her anguish by refusing to acknowledge she had felt uneasiness towards Raj since stepping foot into his father's Lexus. She surely had been seduced by the devil, she thought. And when his message arrived with and invitation to spend the evening together, she replied with spite,

"I'm torn."

This, to her, said it all. She was in so much physical and emotional pain that these were the only words to describe her despair. Raj persisted by texting just individual, sexy words, one at a time that left the impression he knew nothing of her pain or anger. She thought it only might sink in if he could see the hurt in her eyes so, went to his home with the intention of telling him off. She also wanted to scold him with righteous indignation and remind him of all the times she had said,

"NO!"

She stepped out of her car and rounded the corner to the front porch where her rage was subdued by candles lit that beautifully framed the stone steps. He was dressed in a suit and tie and had a blanket waiting to wrap her shoulders in. Hungry by now for his embrace, she holds back. She gently mentions her pain. He appeases her by asking a few empty questions. She demands that he imposed a great deal of pain on her which he dismissed with gentle kisses and hypnotic words.

Without even knowing how it happened, Stella ended up in Raj's bed again. Not like a loss of will, more like a black out. He was excessively gentle and loving and spoke to her like she was a queen. There wasn't an ounce of threat to this visit which allowed Stella to become, once again, unwittingly comfortable. He apologized if it was too much and used the evening to win her back.

It was such delicious torture for Stella being there with Raj. She felt every emotion in the entire spectrum for this one man; from hatred and disgust to desire and adoration. It wasn't as if she could simply turn off her feelings for him, as her logic advised. She had never operated that way. She craved him with such reckless abandon that she cast aside her better judgement in favor of the rich passion that flowed through her when with her newly abusive lover.

At the end of the night Stella and Raj sat naked on a blanket on the living room floor. They talked and laughed and boasted about their amazing encounters. Out of nowhere, Raj pointed to Stella's exposed vagina and a big grin crossed his face. Next, a certain deer in headlights feeling poured over Stella and her vision turned into a strange motion that was like the effect of a camera holding still on the primary object while zooming out the background. Then, Raj said,

"One lip."

Stella did not move, blink, smile or react in any way. This moment purely paralyzed her. She didn't know what he was talking about or what he meant and was haunted by the echo of an idea to attack Raj and choke him. Many moments passed as they stared at each other, him smiling ear to ear and her an emotionless, expressionless, zombie. Finally, Raj broke the trance and turned his head to pull on his tobacco pen and only said,

"Interesting."

Stella was so confused. What did he mean? Why did he look so pleased? The questions continued to plague her as she remained still with the feeling of being a fly on the wall rather than engaged in the conversation. The music had turned into only a pumping of the drum in her ear in the rhythm of her heartbeat. Like a scene straight out of *Basketball Diaries*, the sound of the slow and steady beat had matched the speed of her movements. Gravity seemed to have been pulling on her as she made several attempts to lunge at Raj.

Soon their exchange would shift in a way that allowed her mind to reemerge from her temporary paralysis. This change in atmosphere happened so quickly she hardly noticed the return of the upbeat tempo, yet her body was gyrating in an instant to the club-like atmosphere the music offered. In the same instant, she forgot completely why she wanted to charge at this gorgeous man and found herself grinning and moving to the music as if she were a conquering goddess. Not too long after this experience, that left her mind as quickly as it happened, she dressed and went home to get some sleep, of course, in her own bed.

CHAPTER XI

Not a Farsi

On another beautiful Saturday afternoon, Raj sent Stella a request to come to his house and followed up with,

"I have a sexy and fun surprise for you."

Stella loved surprises and couldn't resist the invitation. She had climbed aboard the "never mind" train and her emotions about the unwanted anal sex were silenced in favor of physical indulgence. He truly had some sort of spell over her. In her mind, as long as they could go back to having fun, she was willing to put the intrusive experience behind them in order to resume the kind of fun she was worried she would never know with another.

She arrived and he explained that he had arranged for another woman to join them that evening and she should come dressed up like before to complete the fantasy he had created since she last wore it. This dynamic was quite intriguing for Stella, considering she loved to be at the center of attention. She did not attempt in any way to rush over there that night but instead waited until Raj was practically begging for her arrival.

When she walked in, the two were sitting in the midst of Raj's no longer original backdrop, with pillows and blankets and candies. But sitting next to him was a beautiful Iranian woman with dark hair, fair skin and strikingly beautiful green eyes. He introduced her as Parvaneh then sat back down next to her. Stella took a seat opposite them on the other couch. The two spent some time exchanging pleasantries and just as before Raj requested Parvaneh's opinion of Stella.

"Isn't she gorgeous?" He would ask.

To which Parvaneh would reply,

"She is perfect."

At points, the two would speak in Farsi in front of Stella. She didn't mind. The mystery of their conversations was an aphrodisiac to her. Stella felt again like a celebrity. All through the night Raj would demand Parvaneh's approval of Stella to which each time, with less and less emotion she would respond,

"She is perfect."

When Raj left the room, things turned weird. Parvaneh grabbed Stella by the hair at her ears and stared straight in her face and said,

"You don't have to if you don't want to."

"What?" Stella would question with a confused look on her face.

Did Parvaneh believe Stella was being forced to be here? Other times, and more than once, Parvaneh would say in a way that sounded like a cry for help,

"I don't know what I'm doing here."

This would distract Stella in a way that quickly turned her off. She pressed Parvaneh with a question,

"What do you mean?"

Raj conveniently returned and Parvaneh changed her demeanor in a way that gave Stella the cue to drop it. She did and was only confused even further when Parvaneh repeated these phrases each time Raj left the room. In time, Raj suggested the two women enter the shower together. Here Parvaneh would complain to Stella about Raj's habitual showering. It angered Stella that Raj even gave this woman the time of day when she referred to his habit as "so annoying." She hoped for his sake that this Iranian woman wasn't close to his heart.

They returned to the living room to resume the exotic threesome. The three of them played well together. Stella doing her best to be on the the cutting edge of sexy for this man she adored. They were all entangled and moaning and giggling in ecstasy and Stella continued to keep an eye on Raj for confirmation of his satisfaction.

Suddenly, Parvaneh fell ill. She ran for the bathroom and all at once Stella felt a recurring theme. This time, she was in Banu's shoes. Raj went to Parvaneh's side as he had for Stella when her alcohol intake took a nasty turn on her birthday. She joked with Raj about this and expected a laugh but instead was met with much defense and she wasn't sure why. Stella strongly sensed that Raj wasn't very nice when things didn't go his way and so she did her best to explain her comment in a more humorous light for him. This appeased Raj and she was again in his good graces.

Stella knew Parvaneh would need some time. If they were anything alike, Stella thought, it could be a while so she made her way into the kitchen with pot and a pipe. She stood at the sink and began to selfishly toke a fair amount into her lungs. She didn't like Raj's pipe. She couldn't ever get a good hit. As she stood there leaned over the sink, Raj came up behind her and without a word stuck his erect cock inside of her and the two became involved in a somewhat silenced version of themselves while he generously rammed himself deep inside her in the sexy kitchen atmosphere.

Out of the corner of her eye, Stella saw Parvaneh half-dressed and gathering her things and so Stella turned her head to warn Raj and insist that he not let her leave. Stella was certain Parvaneh was too drunk to drive. Before she could make the request, Raj was at Parvaneh's side. He grabbed her arms and they began to argue in Farsi. The longer they spoke, the louder they became until it appeared to Stella that Raj was yelling at Parvaneh and she was begging him to let her go.

Stella snuck into Raj's bedroom to hide from their interaction that had suddenly begun to feel very familiar. She found herself sitting on the floor beside the bed with her knees tucked up under her. This is the position she would take as a child when

72

listening to her parents wildly argue with one another. Naked and vulnerable, Stella felt just like a child and became self-aware again only when Parvaneh darted past her, back into the bathroom. She looked into Parvaneh's eyes for any sort of read on the situation but had only received a blank face from her before locking herself back in the bathroom.

Stella tip toed out of the bedroom and Raj greeted her with apologies.

"Are you arguing?" Stella asked

"No, she's drunk and keeps trying to insist on leaving and I keep telling her it is not safe."

He apologized again and again and then said he should go check on this woman who was supposed to be an acquaintance. Stella slipped on her top and sat down with her phone for entertainment. The longer she sat alone, the more her green eyed monster would rise up. She began to connect to the idea that this woman would be sleeping in Raj's bed with him tonight. An act she secretly wanted reserved for only her. But just as he had cared for her, he would be doing the same doting on this beautiful Iranian woman and holding her hand all through the night.

The jealousy became too much for Stella and she stood up to dress and to excuse herself from this adult party that had gone south. She had her keys in hand when Raj entered the room.

"I should go." She told Raj. "She isn't getting better anytime soon and I'll bet she will be more comfortable if I go."

Raj did not argue with Stella. He did not attempt to change her mind. As she walked to the door he said to her,

"I wish you would stay."

"Why, so you can yell at me too?" She retorted as she left angry and disappointed. At home, Stella climbed into her bed immediately. She was on the verge of tears. Lying there she began to realize that her encounters with Raj were ending badly more and more often. He texted her suddenly,

"The Stella I know would've said, "How can I help." Not, "I should go." Well, life is good, hope you had fun!"

Stella was desperate to be heard by him,

"You don't know me at all." She texted back,

"I left because it hurts to know that she will sleep in your bed tonight."

Raj responded,

"You are so wrong..."

"I'm not wrong. She's drunk and you are a perfect gentleman and would never let her leave." She replied.

"Good night!!" Raj sent back and with that Stella then decides to shut down her phone and gave into the tears. Because she does, she misses his demand for her return. When she sees this in the morning, she tries again to explain her feelings - of which he dismisses -and instead informs her Parvaneh left a note apologizing and that she wanted to make it up to them.

"You don't hear me at all do you?" She demanded.

"I do! I do!" He replies.

He asks her to remain kind and confident and shuts down their communication with,

"Let's talk soon and be sure we're on the same page."

"The same page?" Stella scoffed under her breath, because she recognized that they weren't even reading the same book. Stella melts into the pain of her now completely raw emotions and drops her phone to the floor.

CHAPTER XII

Exodus

Stella had been using Raj to escape from real life. In reality, she had dropped the ball on her new business and because she had miscalculated for a major event and was overwhelmed by competition, her funds were now in the red. With rent past due, it wasn't such as surprise that she received an eviction notice. Stella fell flat on her face and for at least two solid hours she sobbed into the floor, weak and unable to move. What was happening in her life? Why couldn't she figure it out? She believed with all her heart that she wasn't meant to be caught up being someone's employee but had also failed at being her own boss.

Hell, she had failed at being in charge of her own body. From her core, she cried, because her entire life was shattered. When she finally scraped herself off the floor, she called her sister in Oregon and asked for help.

"I don't have money to send but if you can get here, you have a place to stay."

Her sister said encouragingly.

Stella looked around the apartment that had been decorated with a hodge-podge of items she had only collected since her divorce. The rummage for any important, sentimental items only took a few hours since she had always been careful to keep much of those things together. Stella had moved a lot in her life but early on she learned that if you had things worth hanging on to that you had better know where they are at any given moment.

Next, she took pictures and posted her large furniture for sale on Craigslist. Then, she put together clothes she didn't use and all her kitchen and bathroom gear in a box and donated it all to The Goodwill. This left her with just a few boxes and bags, enough to stuff her car with room to spare. She used the money from selling her furniture to fuel her car for her new adventure.

Now that it was truly happening, Stella decided to call Raj. She left him a message begging to speak to him, that it was important but that it didn't have anything to do with the other night. As Stella continued to pack, Raj rang her phone. She picked it up in a panic hoping he could hear the sincerity of her words in her voice. She told him that she had to leave town in the next few days and asked,

"What is it you need from me?"

He asked in a cold tone.

"I don't NEED anything from you I was just hoping to see you before I left." She offered.

"When in your last day?"

"Sunday, well, technically I leave on Monday."

And Raj uncharacteristically clicked his teeth and let out a heavy sigh and retorted,

"Stella, everything with you is always an emergency. I, I...I just don't care for that. So, no, no, I am not available." Raj answered.

Quickly changing her tone, Stella's words fell out of her mouth,

"Oh my God."

"What? What is it?" Raj snapped.

Stella's words were slow and deliberate when she responded,

"I've never heard you sound so cold and calloused before."

This time Raj clicked his tongue like a child who feels wrongfully accused,

"Oh please, you are so dramatic."

76

"So dramatic?" Stella wanted to confirm.

"Yes, dramatic, Stella." Raj hissed.

"OK, Raj." She said while abandoning hope that he would return to the man she knew.

"OK." He repeated.

"Well, bye, then." Stella flatly offered.

"Bonne soiree, Stella." He closed.

She hung up her phone stunned,

"Et tu, Raj?" She said out loud as they ended the call.

She examined how all elements of her life had burst into flames. Now, even Raj, who had been her escape from the bedlam, was part of the madness. The next few days would have Stella walking around in a funk. The project she was undertaking all alone was so overwhelming but because of the trauma that had piled onto her, she was on point with compartmentalization and this, in turn, assisted her with the organization of her forced relocation. She felt as if she made a thousand trips to the dumpster because she continued to come across so much junk that meant nothing to her.

Things had been kept, for whatever reason, were coming out of every drawer and cabinet and every nook and cranny. She thought most of it probably ended up in these hideaways because she had shoved it there in preparation for whatever emergency tidying was needed if company were on their way over. She didn't need most of it and so it would end up in the trash. She did find herself taking meticulous care of the items Raj had bestowed her. Finding a pair of his socks brought about a memory of having referred to Raj as, "You darling man!" She remembers how endearing it was to discover them in her purse after having oogled over how cute they were that entire evening.

It didn't seem long before she was loading up her car with the minimal possessions that remained. Stella cried for what seemed like the entire trip, stopping only to gas the car, use the bathroom or grab a bite to eat. She felt this move was propelled by a life force bigger than herself; or a conspiracy against her. She analyzed about herself how she always seemed to run to others to fix her, though no one could, or would.

77

Stella arrived in Oregon and swore on a new life. She would live a healthy lifestyle, exercise often, eat right and stop sleeping around. She could think of nothing but Raj and the unbelievable affair they had from beginning to end. No one could seem to even catch her eye either. Stella quickly landed a job and spent her evenings working out; jogging around her sister's neighborhood.

About a week later Stella received a text from Raj asking how she was.

"Much better than last week." She answered and attempted to close the conversation with well wishes for the week but Raj continued.

"If you're not busy, you should stop by."

Stella scoffed, "I'm not exactly in the neighborhood anymore."

"?" He responded.

"I tried to tell you but you were so angry at my panic that I guess you didn't hear a word I said."

And like a man going dead on a hospital table, the flat line noise she created with her response was almost audible. Raj finally responded,

"Hope you are well." And, "Keep being sexy."

"You too, doll." She offered while on autopilot.

Without any further pleading for him, she thought she might be compelled to express, he sent a picture of a suggestive masculine plant and she responded with a picture of a feminine featured flower and he sent her a final picture of a sunset. Once this exchange was over, an onset of tears washed over her and she took to her bed to mourn the literal ripping of herself from the greatest lover she had ever known.

That evening she peeled herself out of bed to go for a jog. She began to look forward to these because she would follow the moon the whole way. While her feet pounded the pavement, she would imagine Raj guiding her with the moon. After all, it was his very first gift to her. She would pretend he was coaching her to push, harder and faster as she ran. In her mind, running was the key. She measured her ever increasing desire for Raj by the speed and strides she took. For short distances she felt like a professional runner and his voice lingered in her thoughts,

"Do you want it?"

"How bad do you want it?"

"Come and get it!"

"Hustle!!"

She played like he would holler these things at her and she always benefited from this game. Some nights she would stop, mid-course, and shake her fists at the moon. She had become quite frustrated when her new-found lifestyle and anger began to set in.

"Raj!" She would holler.

"Why won't you come get me?!" She wondered.

She would begin to cry at the idea she might never see him again. On a clear night while out for her evening run Stella rounded the corner and had her breath taken away. The full moon that had been at her back was now on her left and it was as big as any moon she had ever seen. It looked as if it touched the ground and stood as high as a four story building. It was magnificent. Stella stared in amazement.

After that, a strange thing happened. She didn't see the moon again for six straight days. Then, on the seventh day, the moon came out, far away in the sky and was only shaped as a crescent moon. It was a strange and eerie blood red color and Stella said out loud,

"Well, that's a sign if I ever saw one."

CHAPTER XIII

Nightmares

One night, Stella had a horrible dream. She dreamt she was standing outside the kitchen window at Raj's house and he refused to see her. In the distance something straight out of the movie *Beetlejuice*, only the yellow sand in Stella's dream, was breathing red blood. She turned to plead with Raj once more before being forced to step into the hellish atmosphere. Through the window, calloused and uncaring and without even looking at her, he shook his head, "no."

Stella set off into the blood bath and began to cry. The sensation of this betrayal by Raj shook Stella awake, from where she had been crying in her sleep. Stella was surely shaken by this hellish nightmare and continued each night to have these scary episodes.

The next dream, she was arriving at Raj's home again. Her entrance was grand, as she was naked under the dozens of orange and black butterflies that adorned her in the shape of a dress. In the background, the Broadway soundtrack to Peter Pan was playing. Raj- with an angry presence- led Stella to the bathroom and turned on all the faucets, which frightened the butterflies away. This left Stella naked and afraid of Raj.

In a flash, the atmosphere of this dream changed from that of falling to her knees, into Raj's familiar living room seduction scene. In the middle of an exciting sexual encounter, she finds herself on her knees, in the candlelight. She responds to the intensity by grabbing a fistful of material at the top corner of the soft blanket they are on in order to stuff her mouth and curb her reflex to shout in ecstasy. When she does, she spots what looks like a green straight razor. She picks it up, examines it, feels a jolt of fear and so returns it in order to continue focusing on the pleasure of the sex.

The rest of the dream played out on a split screen in an empty theatre as Stella watched. One screen displayed unimaginable pleasure inside Raj's cozy, candle lit room living room. The other took place beneath the setting of a dark night sky; absent of any stars and only a blood red crescent moon hung overhead. This screen followed a grueling nightmare that involved the green razor. Stella woke up in a panic at the climactic reveal of the two movies.

The third, and most realistic dream, was actually that of a memory. She was returned to the evening that she was in Raj's living room on the floor sitting on a soft blanket. He was sitting across from her and they were both naked. They were admiring and complimenting one another when Raj flashed a big toothy grin. He pointed to Stella's vagina and casually said,

"One lip...Interesting."

In her dream, Stella felt like she did in real life; frozen and without any ability to move. She could feel the indignation in his voice, the injustice of the action he was referring to but when, how and why it happened she couldn't remember even though at the same time she knew he was responsible. She began sweating and hyperventilating and tried to scream inside her dream but couldn't. She began to feel as if she couldn't breathe and then she was spinning and spinning and all she could hear over and over as she grew dizzy was, "One lip."

Finally, Stella was able to pull in a gasp of air and woke up as she did sitting straight up in her bed. Sweating and panting for more air, she sat there terrified. Her silent wish was that she had not brought her nightmare back with her. Her panic about it was too great to wonder and she immediately ran to the bathroom and locked herself inside. She stripped naked and looked herself in her eyes in the mirror,

"Can it be?" She asked herself.

She remembered the attempted examination back in California that had come to a screeching halt when her curiosity reminded her she was menstruating. Stella reached down and gently pulled apart the lips on her vagina exposing her inner labia. She squinted and looked again. She ran her finger all around and touched on every part. Did it look different? Stella was pretty sure it was vastly different. She pulled out her compact mirror and placed it underneath her to have a closer look but the mirror was dirty with makeup.

She turned on the sink faucet to clean the mirror and when she did, memories of the night Raj anally penetrated her came flooding back. She remembered how he was so attentive to her after. The pin prick she felt must have been real. That must have been an anesthetic and that is why he massaged the very spot she complained about for quite some time. Then, he told her to go to the bathroom and hold onto the sink while he turned on both the shower and sink faucets. She remembers her confusion when he grabbed at her labia and felt the sensation of a band aid ripping, though she hadn't been wearing one... Stella's breathing became so heavy her chest was visibly expanding and contracting as she connected the reality that this had been her very own labia. Raj had cut off one of her inner labia and also her clitoral hood.

Stella expected a flood of emotion but this did not come. There were no tears, no anger, just her racing heart. Her emotions were doused in the shame she felt about recognizing she had silenced her own inner voice who spoke truth to her and at that moment made her feel as if she had known all along. Stella's stomach turned on her and she involuntarily spent the next hour in the bathroom, violently sick.

She wan't sure what to do next and made a doctor's appointment to confirm that what she saw was really what was there; or rather, not there. The doctor confirmed there was an incision where her inner labia used to be but that it was now missing. Oddly enough, the doctor denied that Stella's clitoral hood was missing. Then, she said she wanted to be sure Stella hadn't been "fish-hooked" - when a hole is cut through the vagina leaving a path to the rectum. Stella felt that this doctor had been curiously well versed in these sorts of checkups. It was as if what she was investigating on Stella was common. In an instant, Stella kicked the doctor out of the room and left the medical office even more angry and scared than she was when she went in.

When she arrived back at her sister's place, she went straight to her room. She fell flat on her face on her bed and screamed as loud as she could into her pillow. She then, used her fist to pound out some anger on it and she began breathing quite heavy and quickly while imagining the pillow was Raj. She took it in her two hands and squeezed it as hard as her hands would allow. She was silent and shaking and glaring with intent and not breathing as drool fell from her lip. It was a scene straight out of *The Shining* as rage possessed her. Loudly and all at once, Stella released the pillow in a grand fashion while at the same time audibly drew in a giant, much needed breath. The panting that followed slid naturally into an outburst of tears.

Big, raindrop-sized tears fell from Stella's eyes as she pulled on her hair and gritted her teeth.

"Why?! Why!?!" She cried over and over for what seemed like an eternity.

"I did nothing to you! Why!!?!!" She shouted to the ceiling. She shouted as if he were standing in front of her.

"I did everything you asked of me! I took it all without complaint! You whipped me to the verge of blister, groped me like a toy, slapped me for shock and even stole my will and forced your dick in my ass; all in the name of desire! Why do I deserve such punishment?! This is not something that is over when the sex is, you mutilated me for life! FOR LIFE!!!" She screamed again at the ceiling.

She pulled at the blankets on her bed and she yanked at the pillow cases with her teeth. She screamed, closed-mouthed, as hard as her lungs were able. Stella's heart was in so much agony; Raj had shattered it. He had tricked her into believing that he meant her no harm and that he could be trusted.

"Who treats someone like this? Why would he cut me?"

She wondered and her wounded heart cried harder when she realized she would probably never know. For 92 hours Stella laid in bed, completely debilitated. She sobbed harder than she ever had in her life because her own primal, survival instinct had failed her. She wondered if she even possessed such a thing. Such misery and shock consumed Stella over his violation of her. Because of yet another onset of trauma, Stella's head was a spinning carousel of images and flashes of a reality that hardly seemed real.

It would be the physical evidence that held her back from convincing herself this was all just a nightmare. In her heart she wanted very much for this to be the case. She imagined scenarios in which she were mistaken and that no alterations of her feminine flower had taken place. Again and again, this trap would lead her back to tears when the reality of the human right of which she had been violated and robbed of, would take hold of her and appear to scoff at her in the face of her humbled moments.

Stella wondered why only now did she remember? She was there and aware and awake during these moments but felt completely without a will of her own. She knows she was never too drunk, she didn't even like to drink that much. Could he have slipped something into the one of her drinks? Then, she recalled times where she would lose sight during their love making and wondered if she had actually passed out for numerous periods of time. The conversation in which he pointed out Stella's single labia continued to play in her mind. That really happened too. Her dream of it was a replay.

She had now reconnected with the memory of it and how she really had felt immobile. In her mind, thoughts of charging Raj at that moment and strangling him were dashed as the recollection of her inability to respond became alarming.

As he said the words, "one lip," bells and whistles rang in her head and she knew it then! Well, some part of her anyway was screaming at her on the inside, yet she was stuck without any control of any part of herself. Stella examined her life then and compared it to her life now. Since she was with family again, she didn't feel so scared for her own survival which she was becoming more and more afraid of before she came to Oregon. Stella recalls living in fear each day and how it didn't allow any time for reflection. Now that her life felt more stable, she had time to reflect about her encounters with Raj rather than simply recover from them.

The longer she was away, the more she began to remember. The power the initial shock had over her would only be the beginning. In the months to come, Stella would walk on egg shells trying to determine if the things around her were real or was she becoming extraordinarily paranoid.

CHAPTER XIV

Engine Search

Since Stella had relocated, she and Raj no longer spoke. She had tried a few times to communicate with him before her recollection of this violent act but had not received any responses. She wondered now what she might do if he ever did try contacting her. The complexity of her emotions started to become overwhelming, causing Stella to take some time off from her new job.

The days spent at home were engulfed in a man hunt. Stella had already long ago done an engine search for Raj and he appeared legitimately stable. Things about him were normal, like his climb up the corporate ladder, according to his online resume. His portfolio was all tidy, complete with a portrait that was reminiscent of the one at her father's funeral; suit and tie, hair parted to the right, a clean shave and an unreadable smile. The picture appeared to have been taken several years ago according to the limited receding of his hairline in the photo versus what his hairline looked like now.

She tried her best to remember his address. When she did a satellite search, his house was only identifiable by the grand leaves of the large tree in the front yard that hid the house, the iron archway that pierced through them and the impossibly narrow driveway. It was always so strange to Stella how this street seemed to be checkered with very large houses and very relatively small ones in between. She wondered if the house belonged to him and did a property search through the county's public records.

She entered the address on the county website and received a request for security clearance. This was unusual to Stella so she cautiously closed out the tab and reopened a new window to search the address. Again, she received a security clearance request for entry. She assumed she had been hung up in the web somewhere and her anti malware was working overtime. Not comfortable making any entries for this strange security request she knew wasn't necessary to enter a public records website, run by the dot "org" portion of the government, she called her sister at work and asked if she had time to check the public records from her office for Raj's address.

Things went from strange to scary when her sister told her that her search returned with a nonexistent address. Stella asked her to look for the address next door. The aerially visible and considerably larger house next door which Stella had not much considered before was owned by a Bahram Raj Safavi. Could this be his father's house? Could the house she was accustomed to be a type of guesthouse for the larger home to the north? She tried to run an engine search for Bahram Raj Safavi but nothing turned up. Only Raj's generic profiles on American social websites; nothing for anyone named Bahram.

Desperate for clues, Stella paid for an online background check of Raj which only found a return and this name. The name of Bahram was not found on anything but the giant house Stella had never stepped foot in. The paid search showed Raj's run-ins with the law. To her surprise, Raj actually had two prior arrests; both on charges of "bodily harm." Both cases were dropped for lack of evidence.

"Well sure,"

Stella snorted in the silence of her room,

"You could hardly break a sweat before that man demand you hop in the shower."

In fact, it made her start to feel quite foolish about falling for his neuroses about cleanliness. Now, she realized he was getting rid of evidence and she had dutifully helped him. Stella grew ill as she realized this also meant that her Godly instinct did work. She remembered how she always felt like some sort of cog in Raj's revolving door of deception. She had experienced that feeling and now she knew why she felt that way; because that is the way it was.

What she wanted to know now was, way hadn't she had the will to walk away? Because this cheap background check had led to another dead end, she embarked on a search for more detail on the things she did know about him. Her first thoughts went to his country of Iran. She remembers clearly the large flag that adorned the inside of his garage, leaving no question to his heritage. She typed the simple word "Iran" into a video search and was led to speeches heard at the United Nations by Rouhani. She listened to a speech he delivered in 2014 wherein the words he spoke rang in Stella's ears, like bells in a church steeple at noon on Easter Sunday:

"Certain Agencies have placed razors in the hands of madmen who now spare no one"

Stella then typed into a search engine this phrase that struck her to her very core. It turns out this line in Rouhani's speech was received, with matched intensity, by the media evidenced by his presence in numerous headlines. But this is the first Stella ever remembers hearing about this. Did people not take this man seriously? She believed what she experienced by Raj is exactly what Rouhani meant. Stella recalled the tiny green blade she saw on the floor and couldn't remember if it was real or a dream. Things were shaping up to imply she was a victim of a new, silent and raging war on the single and vulnerable women of America.

She knew Raj was with numerous women and couldn't help but imagine his home to be quite similar to a factory. She truly had encountered the devil himself. Stella contacted the local police in Santa Monica. They listened to her story and asked her questions in great detail and when she refused to provide her personal place of residence, they placed her on hold for an extended period. Eventually, a man with a very domineering tone came on the line and said,

"I'm sorry, ma'am, our hands are tied. Information regarding activity at that location is protected by National Security. It is unadvisable to pursue this matter, in fact, we think it's best if you cease and desist on your search."

"National Security?" Stella thought.

"Who is this Iranian man?"

She wondered and hung up the phone when a tidal wave of ideas came to her mind like the rushing waters of a broken dam. Back in Santa Monica, Stella had stepped into a man's game of lust, emotionless, strictly physical sexual encounters. She played as hard as Raj did because she somehow thought it make him want her in the same way, even though time and time again, he would repeat that they were just having fun. What if her pursuit of equality had backfired on her? And how many others, she wondered had suffered like her?

Tons of women in America acted in the same manner as she; tramping around to lure in the true man of their hearts. American women have been taught that desire is the key and so they spend most of their time practicing being desirable. What if the mutilation of American women was an order given as part of the terror promised by Rouhani?

Stella wanted to know the culture in Iran and the consensus about the topic of circumcision. It was crushing to learn that at least a third of the women in Iran have been circumcised by the will of their families. What is worse, the Iranian clergy pretends not to even know of its existence. This search grew as answers to questions inspired more questions. Her search seemed boundless and eventually she found herself back in the United States on the topic of what she had learned was officially referred to as Female Gentile Mutilation or FGM.

It shocked and worried Stella that all she was able to find, after hours of research, were laws protecting girls under 18 from their own families committing or conspiring to commit FGM. No laws regarded this as an act of human violation if this were crime being committed by someone outside of a person's family. Did this fall under regular assault? It certainly didn't feel "regular" to Stella but she resisted pressing charges because she knew she had no evidence.

It would be a case of her word against his and how on earth could she explain that she hadn't any recollection of the event until months later? She had also already been told he was a protected man. The odds were definitely stacked against her.

"Clever Raj." Stella steamed.
"Very clever."

CHAPTER XV

American Woman

Ideas poured over Stella about ways to humiliate Raj. Once she passed the irrational violence scenarios, her understanding that her cause could not insinuate insanity directed her to a silent intelligence. There would be no repercussion for Raj, it seemed. This caused Stella to wonder what she could do. If she was truly unable to seek revenge, she had to find a way to ensure that her very own human debasing experience wasn't for absolutely nothing. This set her on the path to something that would turn out to be even greater than she, from her tiny room, could imagine.

The very stigma of sharing her story with anyone was petrifying. It was as if she was feeling a psychological exclamation point that also included an illusion that she should somehow bear some guilt. She heard the voice of her judgmental ex-husband chastising her for acting like such a slut in the first place. Before she had met him she had only been with one other man. Since their divorce, she had burst the doors of her sexual repression wide open and ceased every opportunity that intrigued her. She wondered why, considering all the men she knew who indulged in a lifetime of meaningless sex without punishment, why did she run into such castigation? She had only begun such philandering and had been very careful not to mess with any men's hearts.

She hadn't had the time to provoke the interest of any men beyond the bedroom because she had been too busy prancing to a charmer's dance for Raj. His immunity had prevailed without wonder since it was he who turned out to be the actual snake. Time and time over she agonized about how this could have happened. This brought about a broad reflection of some defining moments in Stella's life.

Her past was littered with circumstances that allowed for less than the development of her individuality. On some occasions, these undesirable experiences left her in a somewhat reverted state compounding the vast canyon between her mind and an identity. Beyond the stifling and degradation, the stealing and insecurity she lived during her marriage, Stella's home life growing up was violent and scary and without security. Stella felt free for the first time after she had divorced but had so much growing to do.

In her world, it was as if she had become a real life Red Riding Hood. Contrary to modern secular belief, Stella was certain The Big Bad Wolf did, indeed, still bite. Stella had tried her best but could not remember much of her life that didn't feel like a pressure cooker. A lot of a person turns up missing when mere survival steals their development. No definitions of themselves can be declared when they don't know how they will gather all of their resources for the next day. For Stella, this survival state had been with her for most of her life and as a result she hadn't come very far on her own definitions.

When her ex-husband entered her life, she had been warned of repeating history by making similar mistakes such as that of her mother and grandmother. Although she felt she had truly put forth all her effort into heeding this advice, the choices she thought were defying history, ended up leading her down the same seemingly predetermined path.

Now, because of her fragile naivety, she found herself the victim of a cruel and violent act. Though she felt alone, she believed there had to be others and she was determined to find them. In the age of social media, Stella knew it wouldn't take long to connect to someone like her. She envisioned a room full of women who have been harboring the result of a similar nightmare. Alone, afraid and without anyone to talk to, because who in their right mind could buy such an accusation?

She wondered if they would be anything like her. Would they come from healthy, stable families? Would this be their first trauma or, like Stella, would this just add to the list? Stella's broken home always had her feeling much like Blanche DuBois, the tragically inept woman who has, "always depended on the kindness of others," [6] which had clearly increased her chances for danger. Stella felt like an orphan sometimes. A daughter of her nation whose consumer culture was driven by the almighty dollar; who's poisoned media had influenced her on a much grander scale than she would recognize in the moment.

Though she knew there were others out there who had suffered as she had, she knew there were even more who were simply at risk. How many other little girls have seen such violence in their lives? The divorce rate that displaces children in a traumatic fashion only grows every day. How many of them watch TV or movies? Suddenly, Stella felt relative to a cow in a herd. Caged and overpopulated with a mass of other zoned out, blind, following cows. And then, she felt a strong desire to scream at these cows,

"You're all headed for slaughter!!"

And all at once, Stella found a new purpose.

"For them!" She realized.

"For all the daughters of our nation; the ones who have been seasoned and kneaded by our mind altering culture and abandoned by their fractured foundations." She said out loud.

She looked to herself. What did she need now that this had happened? More than anything, she needed someone to talk to. She found herself without a soul to support her. There wasn't anyone she felt she could trust. She had tried talking with her sister about it but she could not explain and did not want to create cause for her sister to worry. The topic was dropped and the subject shifted to an idle

---

[6] *A Streetcar Named Desire, Tennessee Williams*

discussion. In this day and age, Stella knew of only one way to purge her anguish; a blog.

She now had a platform to speak on and would use her own nightmarish experience to encourage others to come forward in order to calculate the size of this great threat Stella had discovered that was in need of great protection. She wanted women to become aware of this danger worldwide. She asked others on her new forum to confirm their victim status and see how this number grew. She wanted to bust the lid wide open on this project so other women could have the weapon of awareness. Stella wanted to help what she now lovingly referred to as the "Daughters of Nations," unveil the terror behind the regally dressed men of violence.

Thankfully, due to her job, Stella had a great deal of experience running social media campaigns. She went through several names for her awareness movement and finally settled on "Daughters of Nations Unveil Terror" when she discovered the acronym was D.O.N.U.T. This was a heart wrenching reminder of her once enjoyable company with Raj. It caused Stella to recall their trip to the mountains and how her embarrassing donut revived Raj from an almost imminent, crippling result of his energy drink and liquor elixir that had backfired. He was repeatedly so enthusiastic of the swiftness of his recovery once he ate it.

She believed if Raj ever took notice of her work to begin with would be a miracle but in the event he did, she thought the name D.O.N.U.T. might create enough of an emotional stir in Raj to satisfy her lust for poking the bear. Though she wasn't sure anymore that he even possessed such human qualities. She was diligent, setting up a profile for all the major social media sources with her new cause attached. Each profile explained as delicately as possible the "terror" her cause referred to and each outlet was named D.O.N.U.T.

At the very least, Stella believed she could create a chat space and then she would have others to talk to. As she gathered facts and resources for reference, she found one function that appeared quite large. "International Day of Zero Tolerance for Female Genital Mutilation" was a federally endorsed conference scheduled each year on February 6th. The event supported the elimination of the act

94

everywhere, for everyone that is not of medical necessity. It constitutes FGM as a violation of human rights. Stella wanted to team up with the cause to introduce and further spread the awareness of the threat from her perspective.

The more she focused on the cause, the stronger her convictions became. Stella worked hard and with pride at her new cause. She decided to get with the times and include a video on her website. The video was a seven minute speech about Stella's experience and her growing belief that it was part of a grand scale guerrilla attack on the American woman. As this idea grew, so did the accusations in Stella's video. She became so attached to the belief that Raj's actions were that of Rouhini's words and the speech in her video that promoted her cause reflected this. The words flowed from her with ease and intention as she seamlessly lead the topic from Iranian warnings to American danger.

"If nothing is done in the manner of legal recourse to these men who now invade your American women, it will display to us as an entire gender that you as the opposite gender, the men in power, in fact, condone this procedure and have no plans to eliminate its tolerance."

The feelings behind her words, during the recording, were so real and large to Stella that when she finished recording, she became still and silent in the very implications of her statements.

She wondered, and both reveled and feared the possibility that someone in power would hear her cries. She found herself relying on the voices of others to satisfy her desire for revenge and admitted to herself this was the case. The future safety of others is what she thought she should focus on and did her best to tuck away the seething disgust for the reason she spoke about it in the first place.

"There is a reason this happened to me." She thought.

If she wasn't going to be able to ask Raj the reason he had done this, then she would create one with the movement of D.O.N.U.T. She pressed on, even with her emotions elevated to a dangerous high and posted the controversial video.

CHAPTER XVI

Hello, Goodbye

Six months had already gone by since Stella moved to Oregon and some time had passed since she returned to work. This resulted in the need to lead a double life. When at work, she had to be focused completely on work or else she made time-consuming mistakes. A few of the men in Stella's office had taken an interest in her as well. She adored the attention but wasn't sure she was ready to become involved with anyone. She knew herself to become physical very quickly but how would she explain her new appearance to anyone who might ask?

The fear of this alone was enough to repress any urge she might have had to be with anyone. This resulted in wet dreams. The Philippine man in Operations, who was also in the Army Reserves, showed up in her dreams one night to relieve her of her tension. When Stella returned to the office the following day, she heard word that the Philippine man had been activated in North Korea. Stella always thought this was strange since no conflict was occurring in North Korea.

Another skinny, curly, red headed young man who worked one floor up struck Stella's attention one day, weeks after the Philippine disappeared. They found themselves in a short walk to the break room on the third floor. She was pleasantly surprised when he followed her into the stairwell rather than taking the elevator. As they reached the second floor platform, he called her name, stopping her in her tracks. She spun on her heels to face him and before she could even lift her eyes to look at him, he pressed her up against the wall with his whole body and lifted her arms over her head by her wrists. He grinded his pelvis into hers several times while bouncing to give the image that he was fucking her.

Although this took her completely by surprise, she thought he was attractive and she was overwhelmingly horny. It was then that she noticed the security camera in the corner but rather than protest, she let out an audible breath of pleasure to relay her approval. When they left the stairwell, they parted ways without word or even eye contact. Stella decided against the coffee she was after and walked back to her desk careful now that her undergarments were soaked in the absence of satisfaction.

Later that week, the curly red head waited for Stella in the parking lot after work and invited her to have a drink with him. She agreed and followed him to a nearby bar. The loud and loveable office clown showed up within minutes of their arrival and joined them. Stella was glad this had happened so she didn't feel bad excusing herself during their first round of drinks to take a call from Raj. She left a twenty dollar bill on the bar and got in her car to answer the phone. Her heart pounded and tears welled in her eyes. She did not know if she was frightened or happy to hear from him.

A thousand thoughts crossed her mind as the phone rang again. She was afraid to answer and afraid to ignore him. She finally picked up,

"Hello?"

"Hey sexy doll, how are you?" He opened.

To her surprise, she engaged in a typical conversation with Raj as she drove home. She pretended nothing even happened. She felt this would offer her better opportunity for her surprise attack if she did have the chance for revenge. All these commando precautions she considered, however, went out the window when he began speaking to her. His intoxicating baritone voice coupled with his Persian accent and lip service decorated in wit, proved to be too much for Stella's defense.

"I'm amazing, how about you?"

"Oh, terrific! Enjoying life, you know." Then he interjected,

"I've got to tell you, no one has touched my dick since you left."

"No?" She questioned.

"No, no, seriously, babe, no one fucks me like you do." He lathered.

From where Stella stood, these words appeared transparent. She knew his active sex life hadn't come to a screeching halt because she left. He laid it on thick boasting of her talents and skills in the bedroom and how he had never met anyone like her before.

"When are you coming for a visit?" He asked.

"My visit is... tentative." She responded, not making any commitments to him.

Stella never allowed the conversation to extend beyond small talk and soon made her move to get off the phone. When she did, Raj made an unusual proposal to Stella,

"Do you want to be my exclusive whore?" He spat.

"Well, sure, that sounds sexy." She automatically replied.

"Do you want to be my exclusive whore?" He repeated.

"Yes, yes!" She followed.

"Say it, say the words, *I want to be your exclusive whore*." He instructed.

Refusing to follow instructions she replied,

"I am! I already am your exclusive whore."

Then they said their goodbyes and hung up. Stella went to bed that night contemplating Raj's intentions. He knew he cut her. What did he still want with her, really?

The next morning at work, word spread that the curly headed guy on the next floor had been in a terrible car accident last night when his breaks in his car failed and he flipped into a field. He survived with a broken arm and leg, bruised face, sliced ear and a patch of his head had been scalped on the concrete as the car flipped.

Stella was stunned and felt swollen with emotion for him but not even a dangerous car accident could retrieve Stella's attention from the thousand mile distance that remained with the mystery of Raj.

The following Saturday, a man at the mall expressed interest in Stella while she was out shopping. He introduced himself and asked for her number. They parted ways but saw each other from time to time as they lapped the mall and each time would stop to talk and stand inside the intoxicating space of their electric chemistry. Once she left the mall, she never heard from him and though she may have thought this weird, it seemed to be her luck since she had moved to Oregon.

She didn't begin lumping these scenarios together until one evening at the book store, out of the blue, a man walked in and struck Stella a little so that she gasped. He looked right at her and just smiled. They played cat and mouse in the aisles until finally she approached him and she asked his name. They exchanged numbers and he left before her. He called her phone to give him her number but then never called again. And what weird luck it started to seem to Stella, but she truly didn't care. Her time and energy- and growing anger- was poured into promoting D.O.N.U.T

CHAPTER XVII

Daughters Beware

Stella's video was picking up steam. A popular, alternative and highly controversial web show sent Stella an email about her video and invited her to do a telephone interview during one of his live broadcasts. The host had picked up wind of a claim that the current threat ISIS had received orders to enforce the practice of FGM; an order that was said to have affected 4 million women. The host was interested in Stella's story to fuel the fire on the outlandish message the UN had reportedly delivered.

Stella was delighted to receive advertising for her cause with such a popular webcast. This way, she would be able to advertise the campaign she had envisioned running when her organization came to mind. Stella thought now perhaps she would make a legitimate impact with the publicity the webcast provided. Her growing credentials would surely help her find a way to make it to the Zero Tolerance Conference; a goal she had first set at the inception of D.O.N.U.T. She mentioned during her interview that D.O.N.U.T. hoped to be a strong presence for this year's event. Privately, she hoped it would be the interview itself that landed her in the position she was after; speaking for worldwide media coverage on her discovery of an Islamic Extremist sick plot.

It did not take long after the interview for Stella to receive her invitation to the 2016 Zero Tolerance Conference. There, she would be provided with a worldwide, television broadcast to millions, while she spoke among the thousands who would attend the event. She was confident that when word got out about the threat the country's women are facing, the men of the nation would rise up in defense.

When the event arrived, Stella was prepared. She felt strong and empowered and proud to be walking the path of her destiny. She was ready and willing to become the face of warning to women. The months that had passed since she discovered her own mutilation had been spent focusing on the safety of others. This act of human kindness surprised even Stella considering the circumstances.

The day of the conference, she stood in the left wing of the large outdoor stage. She peered out at the crowd. It stretched from the pit to the top of the hill at the back of the sprawling lawn. The speaker before her was a young girl from Africa who had been "vacation cut." This is the practice of convincing a young girl she is traveling to her native country for vacation when in fact the purpose of the trip is to conduct on her the procedure of FGM. The families will typically send a girl to her native country in order to avoid violating laws constructed against this inside the United States. Stella's eyes filled with tears at the girl's recount of her PTSD[7] induced experience.

A lady with a headset rushed up to Stella and raised her eyebrows as far as possible to emphasize her seriousness while she spoke very deliberately to Stella about being ready to go on when the girl was finished. She instructed that she should try not to take too much time because a large crowd like this becomes restless very easily and she was in charge of preventing the need for crowd control. Then, she asked if Stella was nervous. She claimed she was not but inside her were a million wild butterflies.

"You'll do great, remember, speak loudly and get

---

[7] *Post-Traumatic Stress Disorder*

the crowd involved! Good? OK. Keep an eye out, someone will signal you when to head for the microphone."

The woman never waited for any of Stella's responses before rushing away with as much attention as she could draw to herself about the idea that she was coming about to bark orders at everyone. Stella began to practice her speech under her breath and arrange her notecards for easy prompting. Just then, she felt someone grab her arm. She whipped around to engage her intruder only to be stricken with an overwhelming amount of emotion as she realized she was face to face with Raj.

"I need to talk to you." He said firmly.

"What are you doing here?" She demanded.

"You're making a mistake." He pressed.

"My only mistake was allowing you to seduce me." She growled.

"You don't mean that." He replied with a most gratifying hurt in his voice.

"Yes I do, you son of a bitch." She continued.

"Stella.."

"YOU CUT ME!!!" She screamed but the place was so loud it was only for his benefit.

"Yes, but..." He tried but Stella cut him off.

"WHYYYYYYY, would you do that?"

"Please listen to me." He tries again.

"I can't Raj. I'm busy saving thousands of women from the same humiliation you thrust on me."

"Oh Stella, always with the drama. Now, please stop shouting at me and listen. Please?"

Raj grabbed ahold of both of her arms and looked directly into her face. She had nowhere to go. With her lips pursed and her chest heaving, she held her silence to hear him speak.

"Thank you. Now, I understand you're upset but what you are claiming here is all wrong. You have taken a private event and used it to vilify my entire native country."

"A private event?" She repeated in disbelief.

"Yes, a private event." He mimicked.

"But it was your president who stated blades had been placed in the hands of madmen..."

And Raj interrupted,

"Rouhani was speaking about Islamic Extremists. I'm Zoroastrian. Feminine circumcision is not about war and torture to me and my culture. It is about health and pleasure."

"I appreciate health and pleasure, Raj, but I am an American woman! In MY culture what you've done is assault." She countered.

"Stella, please don't think of it like that. Think of it as an honor, that I chose you and how you are worthy." He insisted.

"Worthy? What does that mean? And what did you do to me that separated me from the pain or will to even fight back? And why is the activity at your address classified? And why can't I find out anything about you "Bahram," who are you?"

When Stella rattles off these words, he realized that she's done her own investigating and there is a genuine shift in Raj's answer. Calmly, he takes a deep breath and then answers,

"My name is Bahram Raj Safavi. I am an Iranian man who works for your American CIA. Because of my training, I have access to certain mind control techniques. I learned very early that you were highly suggestable and when I realized I would have a hard time letting you go, I knew my culture would demand your circumcision if I ever wanted to integrate you into the rest of my life. I know quite well that you are a stubborn American woman and would never have agreed to something so far outside of your culture that could have potentially kept us apart."

Stella was dumbfounded. All she could manage to verbalize was,

"Wha?"

Raj continued,

"I am sorry if my actions have caused you such despair, but you must put an end to this. If you go out there and speak to all these people and the millions watching worldwide making these accusations against Iran of a guerrilla warfare that does not exist, you will tarnish the trust our governments have come to gain for one another. Please, don't do this. This has the potential to become much bigger than you realize...please."

He pleaded and then Raj turned and walked away leaving Stella in the wings, her eyes gazing off in the direction in which Raj had wandered. A white noise fell over the crowd and only a ring remained in Stella's ears as she considered Raj's words. It occurred to her in that moment that though she continued to be diligent and active at her cause, her request for a community of like survivors had not sprouted quite as quickly as she assumed it would. Still, Stella had come to feel so responsible for protecting young women against harm that she was being told didn't exist.

Just then, the announcer at the microphone introduced Stella and D.O.N.U.T. Caught off guard by her cue, her feet stood planted where she was as her eyes darted repeatedly from the stage to her notes to the direction in which Raj had walked away and back again. For several moments, Stella remained paralyzed. All of a sudden, her life was turned upside down again and just as quickly as Raj had appeared. In an instant, nothing made sense; right was wrong and black was white and evil was good.

Her delay prompted the announcer to call her again at which point the lady with the headset came rushing toward Stella, wide-eyed with panic. Her arm was thrashing toward the stage as she pointed toward it with her pen still in her hand. Stella could feel the sense of urgency all around her and yet could not move in the direction she had been headed for several months.

The world seemed to fall into slow motion as the lady with the headset closed in on her. Stella's heart pounded, her breathing was heavy, her eyes welled with tears and her palms began to sweat. Stella had done what she set out to do and that was create an entire movement to prevent the very action she associated as a dark, political effort. But what if she had been wrong? What if Raj was speaking the truth? What if these implications did have the potential for international destruction but were, in fact, simply a private affair? Seconds remained before she would encounter questions regarding her delay.

She didn't know what to do and wished she could disappear. She was ready and willing to be the face of warning for a brutal and horrific maneuver of an organized terrorist group. But if it turned out that she is wrong, who could forgive her for creating such an unnecessary rift between her country and the native country of her Persian lover?

www.ingramcontent.com/pod-product-compliance
Lightning Source LLC
Chambersburg PA
CBHW060335260626
47160CB00007B/2797